MW01517477

Published by Z. F. Sigurdson

www.zfsigurdson.com

Edited by Adam Petrash

Copy Edited by Emma Skrumeda

Cover art by G. M. B. Chomichuk © 2021

Cover design by Chloe Brown © 2021

First Edition: May 2021

ISBN: 978-1-7771362-3-9 (paperback)

ISBN: 978-1-7771362-4-6 (ebook)

◇ THE VEILED SAGAS ◇

Black as Night

For the dark places we hide in order to find the light

Contents

♦

Beyond the Veil, through space and time, is a realm undreamt of. A place with the glowing eyes of a sorceress and the quaking wails of titans. The forgotten oaths of failed warlords and double-edged promises of cyberspace. A realm of monsters and magic, of blades and bullets, where kings and heathens rule.

Through the Veil, you have entered the Wrong Side.

Nothing is right anymore.

These are *The Veiled Sagas.*

♦

LOST IN PENN VALLEY

A storm rumbled outside, light flashing through the windows and casting shadows across Pak's workshop. The tables and benches were piled with the gremlin's scavenged components and jerry-built electronics. A small television flickered with each thunderclap, interrupting the screaming of a blonde, monster-beset damsel-in-distress.

Min slept better than she had in months after signing on with Pak as his scavenger. Her face was a small circle in the blanket laid over her. She had found safety from the bounty hunters that followed her through the countryside of NeoAnglia.

The street outside was a mess of mud. The thieves, killers, and gangsters that plagued Penn Valley had taken cover.

Lightning flashed again; a man stumbled from door to door, knocking and crying for help.

A door flew open. A deep voice growled. "What the fuck do you want?" A bearded lycanthrope emerged onto his stoop. His wolfish face was lined with bristly grey fur and his claws gripped the doorframe.

The man stood frozen with terror. He didn't respond, shocked at the sight of the not-quite-human creature.

"Get out of here! Crazy human!" The lycanthrope shoved him off the stoop and down into the mud.

"What is it?" called a voice from inside. "Can we eat it?"

"Maybe," the beast's yellow eyes narrowed. "Not worth it. Pathetic." The lycanthrope slammed the door. The man stumbled back into the alley and managed to stumble into a sheltered spot behind Pak's workshop.

He was lost.

Far more lost than he could possibly imagine.

◆

By morning, the streets were filled with puddles of water and tendrils of mist. The gloom of NeoAnglia's weather was inescapable. Pak Milkhide walked down from his apartment loft wearing child-sized overalls and a greasy shirt. His flat bat-like face yawned, revealing rows of needle teeth. He scratched behind his wide ears with long spidery fingers.

He saw Min snoring quietly. Her face looked so small in the nest of blankets, almost child-like—made it hard to believe that she was perfectly adept at violence. The human woman, Min, was a decent worker and a proper fighter. She hadn't robbed him, *yet*.

He went through his usual checks for damage after a storm. His sleepy mind went through the fuse box, wiring, and power. He had to be particularly careful, many of the components would be difficult to replace. The local gang, an alliance of brutes and enforcers under the control of Boss Luka, had control over the generators that powered the town. Whatever coal and fuel could be scavenged and found was what kept the lights on. As long as you paid your tax you had power. It was a rare commodity on This Side of the Veil.

Pak was, mercifully, left alone for the most part. Half his income came from fixing the damn power grid and other odds and ends. He was the local technician and a vital part of the town. As hated for his privileges as he was necessary for his skills.

After confirming all the fuses and wires were fine, Pak headed to the back alley to gather firewood for the stove.

A wood stove was far more reliable than an electrical version in Penn Valley. It was before dawn, the light peeking through the alleys of the gang town. His barred door clattered. The alley leaned in around him as he went to the pile and gathered some pieces from the wood shed. His small boots sloshed in the mud.

When he turned back to the door, he was face-to-face with a human. The boy's face was frozen with fear, his brown eyes wide.

A pair of screams echoed through the alley.

♦

Min jumped out of her sleep and burst into the alley with her sword and revolver in hand.

"What is it?"

Pak was sitting in the mud, rubbing his head. "Fucking human."

Min saw someone running out of the alley. Her protective urge was sent into full swing. Pak had been good to her. She bolted after the attacker, weapons swinging in each hand. *It's too fucking early for this.* She swerved onto a wider street. It was still early; there was still a thick misty gloom throughout Penn Valley.

She heard running and panting coming from down the next alley. Min pursued. He wore a grey hoodie and jeans. *Must have a knife or something*, she thought. The two of them swerved through the dark and dirty alleys. He seemed to run without any rhyme or reason. *Amateur.* The crime-infested town was a dangerous place. Mistakes were rarely met with mercy.

Min broke off down a side alley and circled around, then launched herself at the young man. He tumbled into a garbage bin, spilling trash everywhere. He scrambled backward on his hands and feet, but froze when she held the tip of her sword to his throat. "Hand over what you—" Min paused.

He was a young Black kid, barely into his twenties. His round head was topped with a scruffy fade. The kid was looking at the sword like he had never seen one before in his life. Across his hoodie read *University of Pennsylvania.*

"Please," he whimpered, holding up his hands. "Please. I didn't know. I didn't mean it."

He was absolutely terrified. Min lowered the weapon. *He* has *never seen a sword before, not a real one*, she concluded. "Where are you from?"

"Brunswick, Maine. I got into a car crash. I…I don't know where I am."

Min sighed, exhaling her frustration. *It really is too early for this shit…* "Get up. You're coming with me." She held out a hand. "We'll get this sorted."

He didn't take her hand, but got up on his own, brushing himself off. "Where am I?"

"Penn Valley," said Min. She stood just a hair shorter than the kid

"Where the hell is that? I was just off the I-95."

Min opened her mouth, but another voice cut her off from down the alley. "Hey, you!

She turned, shoving the young man behind her. Her sword hung loosely at her side, but was still ready.

Two figures stood in the alleyway. *Shit*, thought Min. A red-haired Marklander and a snorting wyrboar approached. The Marklander had a bandana wrapped around his head, covering the eye Min had destroyed the previous week.

"There you are!" said the Marklander. "You ain't going anywhere, you fucking bitch. You blinded me!"

A pair of blades slipped into view, glinting in the morning light.

Min dropped into her fighting stance, her black longsword at the ready. "I'm waiting."

They charged. Metal clanged and grunts followed. The Marklander was quickly disarmed and thrown headfirst into a wall, knocking him out. The wyrboar attacked with heavy, clumsy swings. Min slid back and swung; the blade met his meaty arm. His severed hand, still gripping his weapon, fell to the ground. The wyrboar squealed, spit flying off his stunted tusks, and clutched his wrist. She kicked him into a wood pile.

The kid from Pennsylvania had watched the entire brutal exchange with the horrified fascination of seeing a car accident. His jaw hung open, his eyes moving from the severed hand to the injured abhuman. Min grabbed his shoulder and shoved him forward. "Come on."

♦

The door of Pak's workshop clanged open. The gremlin had gotten breakfast ready, a bruise on his wrinkled head. The skillet sizzled with bacon, eggs, and mushrooms.

The gremlin turned. "Did you find—"

The boy's gaze met the bug-eyed goggles wrapped around Pak's bald spotted head. The kid screamed and fell backward, almost tumbling out of the workshop. "What is that?" he screamed.

Min growled and hauled him back to his feet with one hand. Her arms were as hard as metal cables, crisscrossed with pale scars. "Apologize."

"What?"

She shoved him forward. "Apologize."

The boy looked Pak up and down. The gremlin grinned with a needle-filled smile, loving every second of the human's torment. He could either be offended, or enjoy the ridiculousness of the situation.

"I…" He looked at the terrifying warrior woman. "I'm sorry."

"Apology accepted, human," snickered Pak. "Would you like some breakfast?"

The kid rubbed his eyes. "Am I dreaming?"

"You wish," said Min. "Sit down."

The kid sat on the couch with a hunched posture. Min could see he was still scared. More scared than he had ever been in his life. Min crossed over to Pak and whispered in his ear. "He's been Exposed."

Pak's eyes snapped wide. "Oh."

They watched the kid fidget.

"Hmmm…" snorted Pak.

"What?"

"Why is it just humans?"

"I don't think anyone can answer that," said Min.

"Only the gods."

"Oh, fuck the gods!"

The three of them ate breakfast in relative silence. The kid didn't touch his food until Min hissed at him to eat. He would need the calories. She couldn't have him passing out on her. The kid's eyes never left Pak, who sat quietly at his desk scribbling notes between bites. Min shoveled the food in quickly. Light was already pouring through the barred windows of the workshop.

"Where to today?" asked Min, not looking at Pak.

"Junkyard outside of town," sniffed the gremlin. "I think it's time I have you take a crack at it."

Min narrowed her eyes suspiciously. "It must be scavenged clean if it's so near."

"Not necessarily," said Pak. "Be careful on your way there, you'll be passing Lakon's place."

"Who?"

"One of the boss's cretins," explained Pak. "An elf— fume addict, always angry, wants to be king of the valley but can't remove Boss Luka without a fight. He's mostly hoping to outlive everyone else."

"Fuck, fine," said Min. She crossed over to the wall and grabbed her weapons belt off a hook. She strapped it on tightly. She thumbed through her ammunition. *The gods shit in my breakfast yet again.* She only had twenty bullets; ammunition was both rare and expensive in these parts. Daylight was burning and she had to leave.

"You," she pointed at the kid, "are coming with me. I have a job to do, so come on. We'll find you some better clothes on the way." She threw on her bag and her black cloak. The kid hadn't moved. "If you don't move, you stay here with *him*," she snarled. She pointed to Pak, who waved mockingly at the kid.

The kid almost jumped out of his seat; he clung to Min's heels as they left.

The two went out into the street, where life in Penn Valley was carrying on as usual. A gang town didn't have very many nine-to-five workers. There were cloaked figures slinking between alleys trading cash for inhalers of fume. A troupe of Summerset boys with sunrise headbands lounged in a corner playing cards and smoking.

An orc, half-asleep, sat on the side of the alley. The kid stared at the sleeping creature, transfixed by its rugged animal's face and leathery green skin. It grunted and snorted in its sleep. The kid jumped, startled by the noise.

"C'mon!" hissed Min.

They hurried around the block toward a wider street. At another corner they passed a half-naked Celtic ascetic.

His skeletal frame was covered in swirling blue woad and draped in animal skins. He held up a bowl.

"For the gods?"

"Fuck the gods!" said Min. The kid followed quickly behind.

Along the main street of the town were a few surviving businesses. Even a den of thieves needed food, clothing, tools, and the other odds and ends of life. All the windows and doors had bars to deter any desperate thieves, despite most of the shops being under the local gang's protection racket.

Gangster mercenaries watched Min and the kid slip into a seamstress shop. The owner, a vulture-like woman, kneeled over a sewing machine while her granddaughter worked the register. Min purchased a few pieces for the kid—a corduroy jacket, old jeans, a belt, and a pair of boots.

The kid looked insulted. "What's wrong with my clothes?"

"Too new, too clean, too modern," she said, throwing the clothes she had picked at him. "You need to look like shit; otherwise, you'll stick out like a sore thumb. There's a reason the mercs watched us come in."

He nodded. "I'm…"

"I don't really care."

"Still," he said. "I'm Trevor. Trevor Mills."

She looked at him. He was attractive, lean with a long square face. His eyes betrayed his disbelief. He believed this was all a dream.

"You're what we call Exposed, Trevor. That's what's going on. Come on."

"What am I supposed to call you?"

"Min," she said. "Just call me Min."

"Is that your real name?"

She ignored the question and sent him to go change.

♦

With Trevor looking less like he was on a triathlete scholarship and more like he'd stolen his grandfather's work clothes, they set out for the junkyard outside town. Throughout the alleys of Penn Valley, more rogues and criminals were waking up, searching for a few dollars to pay for their breakfast or their next deal. The town was filled with wanted men, women, and monsters passed out in dens and bars, all hiding from the king's justice.

A trio of goblins in peaked hats walked by. Their shrill voices hushed as Min passed. They glared at her with big yellow eyes.

The footsteps behind Min stopped. She glanced back at the kid. He stood, trembling, with his fists clenched.

"No," said Trevor, his legs shaking. "I'm not taking another step until you tell me what the fuck is going on, lady. I'm not climbing a fucking mountain just because a bug-eyed goblin looking thing straight out of Harry Potter is telling me to."

Harry Potter... Min chuckled to herself. *I wonder how those ended.* He had taken the clothes and walked the street like he was in a dream. Now he needed answers. She walked up to the kid and flicked him on the forehead. He yelped. "Still think you're dreaming?" said Min.

"What the fuck?" he rubbed his forehead. "I...I..." He blinked. "I don't know. It can't be real."

"It is."

"Why should I believe you?"

"Because I'm the only one who won't shoot or kidnap you."

He blinked again. "Why is this happening?"

Min took his arm and pulled him into an enclave between buildings, away from any windows. "What's the last thing you remember? Before things got...uh...weird?"

He glanced down, eyes searching. "I was driving.

There was a police cruiser stopping people so I took another turn to get around it. I—Then it started raining and I took a wrong turn. Then I got into a crash trying to avoid an animal."

"What animal?"

He blinked. "I don't actually know. I thought it might have been a deer."

It probably wasn't, thought Min. "Go on."

"I wasn't hurt, but the engine wouldn't start. I tried to call triple-A, but my phone wouldn't work. So, I just started walking, thinking I would find a farm or a gas station."

"Then?"

"Then I ended up in this town. One moment I was by the road...when I turned, I was on the trail. Then when I turned again, I saw the lights of the town." He looked up, his brown eyes pleading. "This has to be a dream."

"You have a phone?"

He nodded.

She checked over her shoulder for spying eyes. Luckily it was early. "Where?"

He held up a small black tablet. She snatched it and held him back as he tried to reach for the device. She studied it, turning it over. *They've gone through a few generations since I've been gone.* She handed it back, glancing over her shoulder for eavesdroppers. "Do not, under any circumstances, let anyone see it. Hide it in your jacket. If anyone sees it, they will either try to buy it from you or, more likely, kill you for it." She was leaning into his face. "Do you understand?"

He nodded frantically. "Can you please tell me what's going on? Where am I?"

"Somewhere in southern NeoAnglia."

"What does that even mean?"

"Hush! It means you're in a very different world."

"But…"

"Here's a question—before your crash, were you having the worst day of your life? Like nothing went right? Like you felt the world was conspiring against you? Everything pressing in to overwhelm you so you could barely see straight?" Trevor looked even more scared, both by her intensity, but also by how accurate the description was. His jaw hung open, confirming everything she had just said. She turned and kept walking. "Welcome to the Wrong Side of the Veil. It's a never-ending nightmare that you will never escape from."

They followed the winding streets through the town. A gaggle of urchins appeared; they swarmed Min and Trevor, shouting, selling, and trying to gain their attention. Trevor was so overwhelmed that Min had to drag him through the gaggle of dirty children. *Nothing we can do for them.* That might have been one of the hardest parts of Exposure. One's modern sensibilities of right and wrong, charity and mercy...all of them were out the door. Modern society, despite its numerous flaws, allowed a level of civility, but on the Wrong Side there was little more than a feudal existence in most parts.

They reached the edge of town;the palisade opened with a wire-fence gate. Along the muddy road stood the once-proud sheriff's office, a wooden hall with a porch and two tree-trunk columns that held up the awning.

In the morning shade, a group of thugs sat at a plastic table enjoying their breakfast over smokes and a game of cards. Three Anglos and two orcs. Min was surprised that they had bothered to wake up this early. A girl with a pained expression handed out plates of eggs, ham, black sausage, and bread. Min clenched her jaw, hoping to just get by before anyone noticed them. The pair walked quickly by.

"Hey," said a voice.

Min growled under her breath. "Here we go."

A tall man stood up. Min was mistaken, he wasn't human. His high cheeks, narrow face, and long pointed ears gave the elf a hawkish appearance.

The elf smiled, lips black as soot, and stepped to the edge of the porch. He wore a long coat with a red velvet vest and cravat. His long platinum blonde hair was tied back. A proper town dandy, Lord Lakon knew how good he looked and wanted to show it. A katana-like sabre hung on his belt.

He's just another thug.

Before he spoke, the elf took an inhaler from his coat and took a long draw. When he exhaled, a stream of perfect blue fire poured out. His eyes dilated.

"Good morning, strangers." He whistled. "How are you this morning?"

"Fine," said Min, keeping herself in front of Trevor. "Is there something I can do for you, Lord Lakon?"

The elf grinned at her manners. Gang towns always had tyrants who were easily flattered. These places were too small and isolated for true NeoAnglian nobility to actually remove them or even care. They had bigger problems and concerns, like preventing the Warwich Kings from nationalising the realm and bringing it into the twenty-first century.

"Road tax," he grinned.

Of course.

Min took a few coins from her pocket and tossed them into the mud. "That enough?" Lakon nodded. "Good. Have a lovely day and a long life, my lord."

She grabbed Trevor's arm and hauled him down the road. He had been staring at the elf. Elves looked plenty human, but somehow hauntingly inhuman at the same time, hypnotic in the eyes and devastating to look at. Lord Lakon grinned as the pair hurried through the gates.

♦

The junkyard outside Penn Valley was a mess of debris that lay at the base of a mountain of solid stone the size of a skyscraper.

"What the hell was all that?" said Trevor.

"Hold on," said Min as she used her knife to pry out a circuit board from its housing. When she realized it was rusted she tossed it over her shoulder.

Min leaned over the pieces of a destroyed dial-up modem. *Useless.* The pair stood in a swirling mess of trash and refuse. It stunk of sour rot and metallic grime, with trash, old equipment, damaged vehicles piled in the crook of the mountain.

Min moved to the next spot and began pulling wiring and spark plugs out of a tractor that had been torn in half. Claw marks ripped into the chassis.

"What was what?" replied Min, finally.

"What was that? The guy with the ears." said Trevor.

"He's one of the local thugs."

"But what about the cops, the govern—?"

"What?" she cut him off as she yanked out a spark plug and put it in her bag. "The army? Police? United States Government? Doesn't exist here."

"Where are—"

"We're just on the border of NeoAnglia, where the Warwich's rule reaches its limits."

"Slow down. Neo-what?"

"NeoAnglia," she stopped, trying to remember how she had felt after her own Exposure. She breathed. "New England. It's a kingdom where you'd think New Brunswick, Maine, Vermont, and Upstate New York would be, but they aren't. We're beyond that now." She opened up a broken VCR and took the circuit board. "On This Side, people have to build their own lives. Some find towns to survive in, some are forced to go on the run, and some, after enough time, build their own societies. Some, like the idea of crowning themselves king."

"Okay, okay," said Trevor. "Slow down. Just let me ask

my questions. Let me get this straight..."

Min moved into the shadow of the pillar of rock that towered over the junkyard. She found a forgotten first-generation Microsoft computer under a car door. She kneeled and began dismantling it.

Trevor rubbed his temples. "Okay, so you're saying there's a hidden world like in all those kids' books."

"Yup," said Min, as she pulled at the CD drive.

"I went through the—?"

"The Veil," said Min."

"The Veil? You said it was because I had a really bad day? But..."

Min's patience was growing short. She slid out circuit boards delicately. "It wasn't a bad day. It was a fucking terrible day and, worse still, you got unlucky. You stumbled into something that exposed you to this world."

Trevor's eyes went wide.

"What did you see last night that made you swerve your car out of the way?" asked Min.

"I thought it might have been a bear, or a moose, or something."

"You said it might have been a deer."

"I honestly don't know."

"It might have been, or it might have been something much worse," said Min. "Welcome to the Wrong Side."

She remembered how the monks of Chateau de Jean had told her about her new world after she had been Exposed. She woke up alone, in an unfamiliar room, with a tray of food and water. Her injuries had been tended to. Everything hurt and she felt very worried about someone. She just couldn't remember who.

Eventually a pair of monks came and explained things to her. She didn't believe them and threw the water jug at them

That night she had tried to escape—

Min's eyes refocused; she was back in the garbage dump in Penn Valley. She froze, cursing herself for being distracted. Her hand dropped slowly to her holster, eyes focused. "Don't move," she whispered.

Trevor froze. *Good. He's smart enough to listen.*

Over his shoulder, a serpent's head hovered a few feet away.

The serpent had an angular head, as big as a wolf's, attached to a scaly trunk as thick and as heavy as industrial pipes. Along its scales were patches of dirt, trash, and chemical burns. It swayed slightly, ready to strike. Its pink mouth opened, revealing a line of crystalline needle teeth.

The head snapped toward Trevor.

Min fired her revolver, blasting the head into a spout of black blood and ribbons of flesh. Trevor yelled. The trash around them rumbled. Four more heads burst through the rubble, all covered in stains and trash like the first. One wore a crown of wires and threading.

They hissed through their needle-toothed mouths.

Min yanked Trevor behind her. She fired twice in quick succession, blasting two more heads to pieces. The headless stumps slunk back into the garbage.

She fired at another, but it jerked out of the way. The two remaining heads swayed, preparing to strike. She fired again, blasting another head off.

The last head swerved and snapped for Trevor. Inches from his face, it exploded. A spray of black blood splattered him. The neck slunk back into the garbage.

Trevor yelped, trying to wipe away the blood. "What the fuck was that?"

Three more heads burst out of the garbage and went straight for the pair. *Shit.* With no time to reload, she switched to her sword, cleaving a head off with her drawing-slash. The other two heads came. She caught them both on her blade. With her free hand she held onto one snake's neck as it snapped for her face.

"Run!" screamed Min.

One head retracted. With her hand wrapped around the other's throat, she forced her blade into its jaw, splitting it down the middle until the blade cleaved down its trunk, leaving nothing but two writhing ribbons. The remaining head snapped and she swatted it with the edge of her sword, chopping off its top jaw.

More heads erupted from beneath as the pair fled. Trevor stumbled on the uneven terrain and Min had to haul him back to his feet mid-stride. She lobbed off another attacking head.

The garbage shifted as more serpent heads emerged. A clawed reptilian hand rose out of the refuse.

An SUV-sized body pulled itself up;, trash tumbled off its shoulders but enough clung to its back to create a turtle shell of garbage. A broad chest held up a trunk of dozens of writhing, snapping necks; a monstrous hydra had made the junkyard its home.

I'm going to fucking kill Pak. "Run!" yelled Min, again.

The pair turned and continued fleeing, jumping over gaps and vaulting over debris. Trevor stumbled again, a pair of heads inching toward him. Min slashed wildly with her weapon, cleaving heads like she was snapping the tops off tree saplings.

She jumped away from a barrage of heads and landed on the roof of a Volkswagen Beetle that sat on top of a hill of garbage. The rusted metal crumpled beneath her boots.

"Go!" she roared to Trevor. The garden of serpent heads snapped at her in a barrage. She swatted at the heads with her sword, lobbing another one off, but whenever she decapitated a head, there seemed to be two more to replace it. They didn't grow back right away, that took time, but there were too many to fight effectively. The hydra's huge bulk charged at her, having grown frustrated with her defence.

She jumped away, sliding down a slope of garbage. The hydra followed with its chorus of shrieking heads.

"Hey!" called Trevor. He held up a clutch of aerosol cans strapped together. He raised them over his head, terror twisting his face.

Min dove away from another attack, jumping in quick succession from one piece of debris to the next. The hydra followed. Its immense bulk slid through the junk, its chest plowing through the trash as a ship would cut the sea.

Min reloaded a single round into her revolver, snapping the cylinder shut. "Throw it!"

Trevor lobbed the cans as hard as he could.

One of the hydra's smaller, still-growing heads snapped and caught the canisters. Larger heads tried to pull it away or bite at the head.

Min aimed down the barrel of her revolver and fired.

The hydra was engulfed in a ball of chemical fire. It's remaining heads enveloped inside the inferno. The air reeked of the vilest synthetic burning smell Min had ever experienced. The surrounding garbage caught fire too. The remaining heads shrieked and retreated into the trash, the hydra churning over and over until it smothered the flames and stopped moving.

They bolted through the valley, escaping the screaming cries of the monster and the reek of the junkyard. Most of the valley was lush and green, with lodges and garden homesteads dotted throughout the landscape. It was the dark and dirty town that ruined the image of the countryside.

"Is…is…" Trevor gasped when they stopped by the trail, "is that a normal thing?"

"Yeah," said Min, coughing and rubbing the smell from her nose. "Most people aren't stupid enough to walk into a monster's territory."

"What does that make you?"

"A desperate idiot." She checked the salvage she had managed to get despite the attack. *It'll have to do.* "Come on."

The kid nodded, looking insulted at her lack of gratitude. *Whatever, kid. There's a lot of shit on This Side. No one cares.* They hurried back through the valley trail toward town. She had choice words for Pak. *Fucking little milk-toast imp.*

"We almost just died," said Trevor.

"Yeah," she said as she reloaded her revolver. "And if we had, we'd get eaten, kid. That is your life now. There are monsters, magic, gangs and bandits in every direction— and that's just the little stuff. There are also despots, invading armies, foreign empires..."

He wiped his face. "You said I got here by coming through the Veil. Maybe there's a way—"

"No," snapped Min.

"No?"

"No," said Min. "Don't even start thinking about it. There's no way back through the Veil."

"But maybe—"

"There isn't!"

He looked insulted. *Idiot kid.* "I can try. I have—"

"No. You can't." She stopped him, pressing a finger into his chest. "There isn't. There is nothing left for you and there is no way back. Smarter people, richer people, more powerful people—they've all tried. If the most connected and powerful wizards in the world couldn't do it, then how could a *nobody* like you?"

"What about those nut jobs that go after Bigfoot or see aliens? That has got to have something to do with this. All of this stuff exists in our mythology and fiction. There has to be a way back..."

"I...I don't know. I really don't. I've heard rumours of partials, people who got a glimpse. I've even heard stories about people returning to our world..."

"So *you* are from the normal world!"

"No shit. I didn't even try to kill you, or rob you, or worse." She turned and kept walking. "And it's called the Right Side, the place we came from. You left the Right Side, and now everything is wrong."

◆

The door to Pak's workshop clattered open. The pair stumbled in, covered in trash and sweaty from their escape.

"Get out! Fucking humies!" Pak howled, covering his flared nose. "Get out! I could smell you from down the road. I don't want a damn thing to do with either of you until you wash up."

"Fuck you! You sent us there! No warning on the big nasty hydra!" Min growled from the doorway. "Hand us the fucking soap, you fluorescent-mayonnaise looking imp!"

The gremlin lobbed the bar and towels as though the humans had attacked him and he was defending himself. "Get out!"

The door slammed closed.

"Come on," said Min.

A stream cut through the town; brothel girls and other locals washed their clothes in the dirty water. Min led Trevor to one of the inns; for a dollar they could use the bath. In this case, 'bath' meant a dish of hot water.

"How can it be like this?" whispered Trevor through the door of the bathroom. "You said this is part of a kingdom?"

Min brushed the lye soap through her hair. Her braid unwound into a long tangle of black hair. She dunked her face into the basin.

"Yeah? And?" said Min, patting herself dry. "It's a poor kingdom with a divided house of lords. Every attempt to unify and become a real kingdom has failed. The king barely has any power and the nobility fight over what's left.

Then you have regions like this, where everyone got left behind. You need to be in a city, either in Franco or in the Underground, but that is a *long* ways away."

"The Underground?"

"The Rocky Mountains are hollow, if you can believe it." She only had stories from peddlers to go off of. "One big subterranean city."

"So, there *are* modern areas? Can't we just go there?"

"To the Underground? That journey's like crossing an ocean now."

"Why?"

"I think it's because our world settled the Midwest before the Wrong Side could colonize it. It's just farmland and small towns for a thousand miles over here; it's *their* corner of the world. Only pockets of the Wrong Side exist until you get further west."

"What about here in NeoAnglia?"

"Yeah," said Min, brushing the tangles out of her hair with her fingers. "I've only been to Plygate and Steigford, but Dunwich and Grandton are also modernized. They've got cars, electricity, restaurants...even a port that brings in foreign goods."

"Can't we just go to one of those cities?"

"And do what?"

Trevor didn't respond immediately. Min began dressing, pulling on a fresh flannel, her old, dirty jeans, and socks worn away with holes. She would need to purchase a new set of clothes before leaving Penn Valley. She glanced at her sword sitting next to the door, eyeing the twin wolves on the crossguard. *Remember who sent you here. Remember.*

"I don't know," said Trevor. "I still don't know if I'm dreaming or not."

Min didn't answer. There was nothing left to say. She finished up and let him enter the bathroom.

◆

It was dark by the time they returned to Pak's workshop. The smell of garlic and herbs wafted toward them. Pak was grilling a pair of pigeons for supper, along with a skillet of potatoes, onions, and mushrooms—a staple for goblin-kind everywhere.

Trevor took his plate. "Thank you, sir."

Pak burst out into high-pitched cackles. "Sir? Sir? Did a humie just call me sir? Ha! Shall I roll out the red carpet? Shall I find the king's jewels? Ha! It's just Pak, humie."

"Alright, Pak." Trevor gave Min a look. "Thank you for letting me stay."

Pak rolled his chair to face the small TV. Min and Trevor sat close together on the couch. They watched a samurai film from the 70s. A warrior was cornered in an alley, forced to draw his blades to defend himself.

After a while, Trevor glanced around and asked, "Is this normal?"

"What?" asked Min, not turning away from the black and white blood splatters. *So cartoonish.*

"Just eating supper and watching movies? After a day of fighting monsters?"

"Has been for the last few weeks."

"Yeah," said Pak. "Before me she was usually shitting in the woods and running from bandits."

Trevor looked at her, concerned. Min didn't meet his eye line. Even if he had accepted that he wasn't dreaming, this could at least be a comforting part.

Pak picked his teeth with a claw. "How much longer are you staying, Min?"

"Not long."

"You're leaving?" asked Trevor.

"I can't stay."

He looked more confused than hurt. "I'm sorry. I didn't know. What...what am I supposed to do?"

"You live your life, that's all anyone Exposed can do."

"I…" Terror melted his smile. He looked like a boy realizing he had ventured too far and was lost in the woods. "I don't know what this all means."

Min slid further from him. She looked the kid right in the eyes. "And that's for you to decide. When you wake up tomorrow, you'll realize this is real. Then you need to decide how you want to live."

"I…"

Min stood up and grabbed her cloak. "I'm going for a drink."

"There's beer in the fridge." called Pak. Min grabbed her weapons. The door slammed behind her. Pak sighed. "She's like that, don't take it personally." The gremlin looked the kid up and down. "You were going to school?"

"Yeah?"

"For what?"

Trevor grimaced slightly, still not believing he was talking to something that wasn't human. He gulped. "Engineering. I also worked part-time as a mechanic."

A devilish grin grew across Pak's face. Trevor probably thought Pak was going to eat him.

♦

Min sat at the bar and ordered a whiskey. She could spare the money for one drink. There was no troubadour, so the patrons drank in shared silence. The small bar was stained black from a thousand spills and the yellowed wallpaper was peeling.

The barkeep was a black-haired man with a bowtie. A third arm reached out of his shirt and picked up a bottle. *Probably a mutation from magic overexposure.* The extra arm moved with perfect dexterity.

Min sipped the whiskey. Her mind drifted to Chateau de Jean.

After the monks had explained her situation, she had tried to escape. Covered in bandages and injured, she slipped through the hallways of the monastery away from the saffron-coloured robed monks. She was as clumsy as a teenager sneaking out their window in the middle of the night. She dropped into the courtyard from up above, her leg almost buckling under her.

Crouching behind a lion statue, she saw into the main hall of the monastery. Dozens of robed monks prayed at a giant, shining Buddha. Light and shadow danced across its golden face. She crept away. She fled through the arched gate and into the night. Only once she got further away from the monastery did she start to suspect that the monks had allowed her to escape.

She ran as hard as her legs would take her. Hills of grass spread out before her. She swung her arms, forcing herself forward even as her legs wanted to give and collapse beneath her. She stopped at the crest of a hill where a tree grew.

"Oh my god," she whispered when she looked up. The stars stretched above her forever. They dazzled like she had never seen in her entire life, the Milky Way like a cascade of crystals on a black canvas. The infinite blue and silver cosmos made her gasp.

"It's quite beautiful, isn't it?" said a voice.

She jumped. Her bad leg gave out and she fell to the ground. She groaned, rubbing her thigh.

In the nook of the tree's roots sat a monk. His robes were heavy folds of red and orange, a huge beaded necklace hung around his neck, similarly beaded bracelets around his arms. His face was deeply lined, but strong, like the knots of a tree frozen in time. Nine dots topped his bald crown. "Are you alright?"

"You can't stop me," she hissed.

"Oh, my dear friend, I wouldn't even dream of it. You're so strong, what's an old man to do?"

"Take me home!" *No.* "Where are…where is…" *They? He? She?* Her mind couldn't grasp the name or even the face. It was like a blur in her memories. She had lost someone in her Exposure. "What is happening to me?"

"As Shifu Hai surely told you," said the monk, "you may call me the abbot. You have gone through an exceptional set of circumstances."

She looked up, tears filling her eyes. Memories of the crash and the attack left her hollow. Whole portions of her identity had been lost in the event.

The old man reached behind his back. He set a sword on his lap and unsheathed the blade. It was a longsword of unreflective black metal. Its long hilt was crossed with silver wolves leaping from a teardrop. He ran his hand across its surface. "I don't know who did this. I don't know who was taken from you or who you were. I wish I did. I would ask the Buddha himself to stretch his fingers and pluck your precious ones from danger and return them to you."

"Where am I?" she pleaded.

"Southern Franco. What I believe you would call Kebec."

"Quebec," she corrected.

"Ah, yes."

"I…I don't understand."

"You will in time, dear one," said the monk. He groaned

as he got to his feet. "Old bones. Time is unkind even as we try to ignore its consequences. Buddha blesses. You have gone through a truly trying experience. Buddha challenges us all. Bless him."

The woman melted into blubbering. She curled up on the ground, hugging her legs, her black hair in a tangle around her face. "Is…is this real?"

"I fear it is." He kneeled next to her. A gentle hand rested on her shoulder.

"Where is my family?" She could only assume she had lost her family.

"I don't know. There is no greater joy in the world than the reunion of family. We are blessed with challenges so we may learn what is the most necessary and what is frivolous."

She rubbed her reddened eyes. "What am I supposed to do?"

"You may stay until you are ready to begin your journey."

She nodded, biting back tears. "Thank you."

"Are you hungry?"

A gasping laugh caught her breath. "Yeah, I really am."

"Good."

They walked back to the monastery, hoping to return before any of the other monks realized she was missing. The night breeze sent rippling waves across the grass. The endless stars twinkled overhead.

A crash boomed in the distance. The pair turned. A shadow drifted across the night sky. A huge pair of bat-like wings attached to a serpentine body flew high in the air. Each flap stirred the air in the valley as the creature headed toward the distant mountains.

The mountains were low, gentle peaks surrounded by rugged forests. The creature vanished into the night.

"This *is* real, isn't it?"

The monk nodded. "I'm afraid so. Let's hurry before it gets cold."

"What do I call you?" she asked.

"Shi Huei."

"I'm…" her eyes went wide, her mind went blank. Her mouth hung open, tongue unable to form a syllable. She couldn't remember her own name. "I…"

"Come. Eat."

They walked back to the monastery. The stranger

was helped along by the monk, who was far stronger than he let on.

Min rubbed her eyes and left the drinking den. She had spent five years with the monks of Chateau de Jean. They were refugees from a long-forgotten war. They had come to the new continent and somehow found themselves closer to the Atlantic than the Pacific. They occupied an abandoned Franco chateau, continuing their traditions and giving refuge and charity as their religion demanded.

Now she walked through the dark alleys of Penn Valley, avoiding the thugs as they moved from one glowing den to another. She passed a girl howling for a client from a second-floor window with her tits out. In another alley, inhuman creatures conducted shadowy rituals for unnamed gods; in yet another men fought over coins.

Min floated between shafts of light emanating from various criminal dens and gatherings. A pair of bodyguards saw her and retreated inside. She hurried back toward Pak's workshop. All she wanted was some sleep. *One more day,* she told herself. *One more day. I'll leave tomorrow night.*

If she didn't set a day, she'd stay forever. Everything was here: money, food, shelter. It was too good, and she needed to continue onward. She was still searching. She felt her sword grow heavier. The swordsmen had just vanished. She had to find them.

She walked across the boards bridging an alley. Sewage water trickled beneath the boards, rising with a disgusting smell. She was just another cloaked figure in the dark streets of the backwater town.

They are better off without me anyways...

♦

The next morning Min felt only slightly hungover. Trevor had passed out on the couch, and Min had curled up on a rug. It was still more comfortable than most of the places she had slept while traveling, and it had the familiar feel of the futon in the monastery.

A hand on her shoulder woke her up. She whipped out her revolver and pressed it in Pak's face.

He stared back at her flatly. "We really need to stop doing this."

"Sorry," she holstered the weapon. Pak started cooking breakfast. The smell of bacon woke up Trevor. The kid sat up, rubbed his eyes, blinking until he realized where he was.

"I...oh," he sighed.

"Yeah," said Min.

He leaned forward on his elbows. He wore a shirt and boxers. She saw how his shoulders sank and his hands trembled. He finally believed he wasn't dreaming, the horrible realization that it was real had sunk in. She wanted to feel bad for him, maybe she did deep down. *It's better he accept it.* Only then would he be able to learn how to live with it.

Min threw on her cloak and grabbed a plate of eggs and bacon. "Where to today?"

"We're going to salvage my car," said Trevor.

"When was this decided?" asked Min.

"When you were out drinking," said Pak.

"You think you can find it?" asked Min. The kid nodded. "Good. I leave tonight."

The others nodded. Pak didn't look at her. "We made an agreement. If he woke up here and this wasn't all a dream, he would stay with me. I could use a trained engineer and mechanic."

"Good," said Min. "Then everything works out in the end."

♦

The pair walked down the gloomy street. The mud-strewn alley had a new interloper, a cackling Eastlander with golden hair and swirling wyrm tattoos. With a shoulder bag, boots, and Pak's woodsman axe he didn't stand out as too modern anymore.

"I have some questions," said Trevor.

Fuck. Fine. "Go on."

He shuffled along with the axe on his shoulder. "So, what's real and what's not?"

"If it's in a storybook or a piece of scripture it'll be real, but not in the way you think it should be."

"That seems reasonable. But...I don't know. I was bad in history. Did the Civil War happen here? What about World War Two? Are there places—" They walked by a blacked-out fume addict. His face was covered in soot and his lips cracked like charcoal. "Are all places like this?"

"I told you there are cities and towns. Some are ruled by local thugs, some by noble families who have ruled for decades—not that there's much of a difference. It's like every time a family gets rich and gets some troops, they declare themselves a noble house with generations of rule."

Trevor nodded. "I—" He paused.

Just ahead of them were two thugs, a human and a satyr. They wore headbands emblazoned with the image of a rising sun. They belonged to the Summerset Gang; both carried weapons in their belts. The saytr flicked a coin up into the air, watching Min and Trevor with whiteless brown eyes.

"Let's go the other way," whispered Min. They turned toward an alley, only to see a burly shadow with reflective red eyes appear in it. They tried another alley, but another figure appeared.

Min drew her revolver. "Get behind me."

"Min," said a voice. "Don't." They turned to find Pak standing with another Summerset thug. The gremlin frowned deeply. Completely helpless, he pleaded, "Please."

"You've caused quite a problem," cooed a smooth voice.

Min glanced around, head spinning. There were already at least three guns trained on her. She had no chance. *Fine.* She holstered her weapon. She exhaled, letting the coin-flipping satyr approach and disarm her.

The voice neared. "Quite a problem."

A thin figure stepped into the morning light, wearing rich clothes and a sword: Lakon, the elf thug from the day before. He looked knowingly at Pak then at Min and Trevor. "Pak, my dear friend, you've been keeping a secret from the bosses. *Tsk tsk.* You didn't tell us you were housing a recently Exposed human."

Pak looked down, ashamed, caught between two irresistible forces: his recent partnership with Min and the necessity of working *with* the overlords of the valley.

He glared up at the elf. "Take us to the boss and we'll sort this out."

"Oh, most certainly." Lakon took an inhaler from his pocket. He took a long draw from the tube, his inhuman eyes dilated, and exhaled a ribbon of orange fire. He clearly enjoyed his position of power.

More gangsters appeared in the alleys and nooks of the street—Anglos, Celts, even an Eastlander and a few Mohawk fighters, backed up by orcs, beastfolk, and others. It was the gaggle of muscle that held the valley in their claws. Townsfolk began to appear in upper floor windows and further up the street, curious as to what the ruckus was about.

Min clenched her jaw, and handed over her weapons.

♦

An overseer lodge had been built above the town in its heyday as a mining earldom. Where once a lord's vassal had run the coal mine, now the town's boss ruled. It was an ugly wooden structure that clung to the rocky face of the hills. Under its scaffold legs was the road that led toward the abandoned mine.

Min and Trevor climbed the staircase to the hall. Lakon led the way with Pak. Behind followed a trail of thugs and monsters. Min looked back over the town. From here the town seemed greyer and more worn than she had remembered with ribbons of smoke, echoes of shouts and voices, and the rising smell of refuse. The gang town infected the green countryside like a tumor, unnatural and sick.

"Hurry up," hissed a thug.

Not now. Trevor wouldn't survive. She wouldn't be able to save him if the violence escalated now. She glared at the mercenary a few places back. He carried her sword and belt over his shoulder.

Min allowed herself to be pushed through the doors of the lodge.

A typewriter clattered away as a small human attendant worked at a desk. The lodge had several small desks. The rulers of Penn Valley were thugs, but they *wanted* to present themselves as overseers. Against the back wall was a broad oaken desk. A ledger that Min would struggle to lift lay open. Behind the desk sat a mountain of pale flesh wrapped in a piecemeal suit and cravat. Boss Luka of Penn Valley.

The ogre's watery black eyes fell on Min and Trevor; behind those eyes was a lethal intelligence. He was built like an oversized child, head too big, arms too long, and immensely fat. Beneath the suit was the frame of a gluttonous monster. He sucked on a cigar as thick as Min's forearm, his sausage fingers set with rings.

Boss Luka blew smoke from his bulbous nose. "What is it this time, Lakon?"

The elf sauntered forward, clearly high off the fume. "I've brought you a gift, my lord." He gave a low bow. They loved to play the game. It was like a child's play, thugs pretending to be lords. He gestured to Trevor. "It seems Pak has been hiding an Exposed human."

The ogre's eyes fell on Pak. The gremlin held the monster's gaze. "This true?"

"Yes," said Pak, flatly.

The ogre rose from his chair. The boards beneath his feet groaned as he circled around to his group of thugs. The human servant didn't look up; she just continued working at the typewriter with regular clicks and rings.

Boss Luka was almost seven feet tall. His pumpkin-shaped head was inches from scraping the ceiling. His eyes wandered from Min to Pak to Trevor. He loomed over the trembling kid. Smoke billowed from between his tombstone-like teeth. "Where you from?"

"Sir," said Trevor, knowing manners were the best thing for his survival. "Brunswick, Maine. I crashed the other night and stumbled into your town."

Luka's eyes went to Pak. "You didn't feel the need to tell me?"

Pak's needle-like teeth were on edge. "He's just a boy. Didn't know if he'd be of any use…"

"*Any* Exposed have their uses," said Luka. "But… dear Pak, you are a valued expert in this. What your assessment?"

"Kid's smart. Engineering student. He's able to handle himself."

"Then it's settled," said Luka. "Pak has a new assistant. Thank you, Lakon." The elf beamed.

No one had a choice in the matter. For all intents and purposes, Trevor was now a permanent possession of Boss Luka and his Summerset Gang.

"Not a damn chance!" said Min.

"I don't believe I was speaking to you." The boss's feet caused the boards beneath him to creak as he stepped into Min's personal space. He blew smoke into her face, an act to establish dominance over the one person in the room he felt he didn't have control of. She knew it and he knew it. Min held her tongue. He leaned in over Min's shoulder; his hot breath sent shivers up her spine. "But go on, miss. You've been working for Pak…doing good work, yes? But you've been causing fights and disrespecting my men…I wonder what brought you to our fair town."

Min kept still and silent. His knowing smile sent bolts of adrenaline through her. *Oh, god…* He knew about the bounty on her head.

Pak was trembling, completely helpless.

"So, we're all clear," said Boss Luka, his voice booming. "You, young man, are now mine. You will work for me and be paid handsomely. You will obey my wishes…otherwise I'll eat you myself."

Trevor gulped.

He glanced back at Min. "Seize her; the price on her head will be useful."

Three thugs moved in to arrest her. Min snarled, ready to fight her way out. Hands reached for her shoulder.

"Wait!" croaked a voice. All eyes fell on Trevor. "I have a car." The ogre furrowed his brow. "And this." Trevor reached into his coat and held up a cell phone, a small, slim brick of metal and plastic. Advanced beyond anything this town had. "Is this worth the price on her head?"

Silence followed. Min's body coiled, ready to explode into action.

Boss Luka smiled, impressed. "Two days Exposed and with sense. You *will* be useful."

The ogre took the phone, the device vanishing into his huge hand. "Scavenge what you can from the vehicle. This will do." He tossed the phone to Pak for study and repurposing. "Now, go. Fail this, and I'll eat you anyway."

"Yes, my lord," said Trevor.

♦

Min and Trevor hurried through the hills toward the south after being let go and getting their weapons back. Trevor had said he came from the south. He hoped so. They went through a pass at the edge of Penn Valley, walking in silence. What was there to say? If they didn't return by dark, they would be hunted down by Boss Luka's thugs; it would be impossible to run from them. They knew these hills and forests better than Min. She knew she could make it out. Trevor wouldn't.

"That was smart," said Min. "Thank you."

"I didn't know what else to do. I couldn't let them hurt you."

Min looked down, her brain rushing for the right words to say. She couldn't form them. She shook her head and spoke anyway. "I've been meaning to tell you something about Exposure."

The pair passed between the charred ruins of an outpost and another cleft of rock reaching up as high as the trees.

"The Veil," said Min. "It warps time and space. I'm sure some scholar knows the exact dimensions, but no one in any town you pass can tell you how far anything is from anything else. I've been walking through NeoAnglia for months. It shouldn't take this long for me to walk from Quebec to Pennsylvania. And I still have a lot farther to go."

Trevor nodded. "Where are you going with this?"

"What do you remember from your last day on the Right Side?"

His brow furrowed. "It was a bad day…like you said." He put his hands in his pockets. "Nothing went my way. I think I had been fired. My mom was having problems, and I was driving to…oh, god, I almost forgot about her. Oh, god." His expression dropped. "I forgot my mom. She needed me and…and I can't be there to help her. And…"

"What's your mom's name?"

"It's…no, that's not it…you know what it's like when you're asked a question and you forget the answer?" His eyes searched desperately for the answer he would soon realize wouldn't come to him. "It'll come to me. It has to."

"No," said Min. "It won't." Trevor looked at Min, eyes glistening. "The Veil warps more than space and time. It warps the people who go through it. It destroys our memories. Not a lot of them, just pieces. The important pieces."

"It really is true? I can't go back?"

"None of us can," said Min. "I know in some places some people have slipped through, but it's always by accident. It's why our culture has always had pieces of This Side. I was once told that the Veil didn't always exist, but at some point, it started growing and only got stronger as the years went by. Pieces of life became myth and folklore on the Right Side, but continued being real here. Then when people from our world got Exposed, they brought some of our technology and culture with them."

"The world used to be one?"

"Maybe."

"And no one knows why?"

Min shrugged. "Only the gods know and *fuck* the gods." Trevor nodded. The full magnitude of his situation finally rested on his shoulders.

He looked up at her. "What did you lose?"

"A lot."

"What happens to everyone at home?"

"I wish I knew."

They walked in silence again as they entered another valley.

From what Min had learned about Exposure, Trevor's family would worry about where he was. His job would call a phone that would no longer exist. His school would wonder where he was. Eventually the police would search, if they could be bothered. He would become another missing person. The truth of it was that he might be less than a hundred miles away, but they would never know it. Eventually, they would move on and forget. Or they wouldn't.

That's what the Veil does, thought Min. *When you're unlucky enough, scared enough, and lost enough, it takes everything. Not just from the one plunged into a hostile new world. It takes everything from the people left behind.*

That's why it was the Wrong Side of the Veil. It destroys everything and no one could control it.

◆

Trevor led them to where he had crashed his car, as well as he could remember. They followed the trail southeast. The trees stretched out in a bowl toward a line of rocky hills, the greenery moving in the wind like the ripples in a pond.

There was a dark line through the forest, a depression in the green: a road.

Min checked her revolver. She had a few bullets in the cylinder, but that was all. She would have to buy more ammo before she left. "You sure it's down there?"

"Yes."

She shut the revolver. "Let's go."

They descended down the slope. Min immediately knew there was no chance in getting the vehicle back to Penn Valley. The trail was too narrow, the trees too thick, and the slope too rough. There was likely no fuel either.

She sniffed. "Hold on."She stepped off the trail and kneeled.

"What is it?" asked Trevor, gripping the axe in both hands. Then he looked over her shoulder and got his answer.

A massive pile of stinking brown dung sat in the grass, flies buzzing above it. The pile was almost a foot high.

"What the fuck could drop that?!"

"Hush," whispered Min. "It's whatever you almost hit with your car. It's still here." She looked at the dung. "And it's big. Come on. Stay low. Stay off the trail."

They crept down the slope, slipping from cover to cover. Min's senses strained to watch the trees. As Trevor followed, dashing from tree to tree, they heard a crash in the distance. The pair ducked behind a log. Min peered into the distance.

Crashes rumbled through the forest.

She saw a shadow stalking through the trees. Its long tail and periscope neck floating as its bird-like legs took long, precise steps. A theropod. The first Min had seen properly since arriving on the Wrong Side. It must have been over twenty feet long, eight feet tall. Its serpentine snout was crowned with axe-bladed crests.

Min felt the sweat drip down her face. She reached into her bag and grabbed a bundle of wax paper; inside was a piece of fermented meat. Its sour reek stung Min's nose and made Trevor gag. She threw it as far up the slope as she could.

"Go. Go. Go." She whispered. They crept quickly down the slope. Over her shoulder, the shadow lumbered in a different direction.

"Was that...?"

"A dinosaur, yes."

"But..."

"Time and space remember? I guess they didn't go extinct here."

They hurried down the slope until they reached a rough gravel road. It wasn't a Right Side road, it was a crude

NeoAnglian trail, covered in weeds and lacking a ditch. If Trevor had turned a different direction that night, he could have remained UnExposed and never the wiser. If only life was that kind.

They followed the road in silence so as not to draw any further attention. After a turn they caught the glint of metal. Trevor ran with the axe at his side. "Come on." He moved toward the vehicle.

Min's eyes went wide and she tackled him into a bush. When they looked up, there was another crash.

About a hundred yards down the road was an older black Toyota Corolla. Its bumper and hood were wrapped around a thick oak trunk. Birds scattered from the trees as a huge shadow stepped into view, each heavy footstep sending shockwaves through the forest.

The theropod was covered in a thick coat of fur-like feathers. Its speckled back shimmered in the light. Its snout flared, searching for prey. It pawed at the ground with its razor-sharp clawed feet. Its crests pulsed red.

Trevor gulped.

Min didn't have more bait. She exhaled. "I'm going to distract it."

"What?"

"Hush. Get what you can and get back to Pak. Don't wait for me."

She left their cover before he could protest. She stood in the center of the road, her shoulders tensed, legs coiled and ready to explode into action. The creature sniffed, its huge, powerful body that of a lethal predator, and glanced in the opposite direction. Min held up her revolver and fired. The sound echoed through the forest. Birds scattered.

The crested snout whipped around, and yellow eyes narrowed on Min. The beast roared. Its jaw was lined with dripping fangs. It charged forward; carried gracefully on its bird-like legs it almost seemed to fly over the ground.

Min dashed off the road. The crashes followed her into the forest, the roars stinging her ears. She ran, dashing like a black-winged insect over rocks, boulders, and fallen trees. If she didn't play it right the theropod would overtake her in seconds. She weaved through the dense trees. The beast followed. Its clawed feet threw up dirt with each bounding step.

She saw a rise up ahead on the far side of the valley, a field of rocks and boulders. Above the trees were several rocky outcroppings, rising like fingers to the sky. She stepped off a rock and flew over a small stream. The beast closed the distance.

She cleared the forest line, feeling the theropod's hot

stinking breath on her neck. She pushed harder. A narrow crevasse opened up in the slope. Min dove and slid into the opening. The theropod slammed into the walls of the formation; debris clattered. It was too large to fit. It swiped with its sabre-like claws. Min kicked herself further into the crevasse, avoiding its reach. She pulled out her revolver and let off two shots. One slashed the theropod across the shoulder, the other bit off a piece of its crest. It roared, its crests flushing from red to a veiny purple.

With a frustrated snort, it lumbered off to find easier prey.

Min waited until she could hear the heavy footfalls vanishing into the distance. She knew she would have to circle back around before returning to Trevor. She brushed herself off and wandered deeper into the rocky formation. Once this might have been the pathway of a series of streams, but now it was a bone-dry maze of megalithic towers and narrow alleys.

Hold on, kid.

Each twist and turn only got her more lost. She tried to keep the tops of trees in view, but it was impossible. She tried climbing up and out of the maze, but the walls were too high and too smooth to climb. Surface runoff trailed through the gravel at her feet and down the slope.

She followed a route she thought might lead to an

escape, but reached only a dead end.

"Are you fucking kidding me?"

She braced her legs and arms on the narrowed wall and tried to shimmy her way up and out. When her head reached above the maze, she could see back down the valley toward the road. There was also a route back through the rock formations, past towers of eroded stones.

A shadow loomed over her. She blinked and yelped, dropping herself back into the maze before the theropod could bite off her head. She hit the ground hard, gravel scraping her elbows. She rolled away from the monster's reaching claws before bolting through the maze.

The beast clambered across the rock formation with perfect avian grace. Its head snapped, trying to reach Min like she was a ferret in a hole. She dove, avoiding another attack. It leaned down, reaching with its clawed arm. She avoided an attack and drew her sword. When its head came for another strike, she slashed it across the snout. It roared as black blood dripped from its face.

Min ran, searching for a way out. She turned a corner, but was almost snatched by its jaws.

She stumbled back as the beast snapped for her again. The creature couldn't quite reach her, but she was cornered into an inlet. It roared, snapping its jaws at her, its crests flashing purple and red, its feathery fur flecked with its own blood.

She looked up, past the crested theropod to the stone pillar above it. At the precipice was a dangerously balanced boulder, only supported by the tiniest neck of stone.

Min drew her revolver. She couldn't afford to miss. She closed one eye and aimed down the long chrome barrel. She exhaled before squeezing the trigger.

The neck of rock exploded just off center. The stone groaned, then fell. The theropod turned just as the boulder came hurtling downwards.

Min ran towards the exit she had seen as a thunderous crash shook the formation. Boulders fell like dominos and a landslide erupted around her, stone scraping and crashing. She could feel the chain reaction of collapsing structures around her. She swerved through the alleys as rocks fell. She turned a corner and saw trees beyond an opening. Debris bit at her heels and dust stung her eyes. "Fuck. Fuck. Fuck!" She dove for the exit just as a wall of rock collapsed where she had been standing.

She tumbled down a grassy slope, lungs burning and eyes watering from the dust. When her vision cleared, she saw a section of the maze had been reduced to rubble. The theropod was nowhere to be seen.

She brushed herself off and hurried back to find Trevor.

♦

Min broke through the treeline at the edge of the road. She brushed the rock dust from her cloak. The tree the car had crashed into was bent away from the vehicle. Trevor wasn't by the black Toyota; she looked around but found herself alone. Her heart began to pound. The doors were open, but she couldn't see him. She rushed to look inside. The axe sat on the seat with Trevor's bag.

But where…

"Fuck."

There was a rustle. Min let out an exhausted sigh. She turned, both of her hands in the air.

Four people stood just off the road: Lakon, and two other familiar faces—a one-eyed Marklander and a one-handed wyrboar. The piggish creature had a sharpened bracer wrapped around his bandaged stump and a hatchet in his remaining hand. On the ground kneeled Trevor. The Marklander held a gun to his head.

"Good day, human," said Lakon with a demented smile. His inhuman blue eyes twinkled. *He's not all there is he?* thought Min. His katana-like blade hung on his hip and Min had no bullets left.

"Fuck off, you pointy-eared excuse for a biped," hissed Min.

"So testy. You know, you should respect your elders. I *am* over a hundred years old. I remember a time—"

"And yet, you never matured beyond a twelve-year-old. How sad."

"Drop your weapon, girl. Your friend here will make a nice technician for *my* town, once I take care of Luka. *You*, however...I suspect there might be a bounty for a black haired Nipponi woman wielding a black sword. And this car! Oh, it's been a good day. Thank you." His demented smile stretched further across his handsome face.

"Drop your weapons," hissed the Marklander, prodding his gun against Trevor's head. The Marklander's remaining eye was bloodshot and furious; he was probably pumped up on painkillers. "I'm going to enjoy taking both your eyes and flaying you alive, you fucking bitch."

Lakon pulled an inhaler and took a long draw of fume. He savoured his display of power.

Min unbuckled her belt, her eyes not moving from the thugs, and reached her hand around to undo the holster. She winked at Trevor. He saw her hand trail behind her into the vehicle, her fingers wrapping around the haft of the axe.

Trevor nodded.

Min smiled at Lakon, moving to drop her belt.

Trevor ducked and Min lobbed the axe into the Marklander. It slammed into his chest, knocking him to the ground. His ribs split and blood sprayed. Min grabbed her sword from its sheath as it fell.

Lakon cackled like he had been waiting for this. He leapt into the air, blue fire pouring from his mouth. He was completely unhinged. Min ducked to the side. Lakon's blade scraped against the car, erupting with sparks. She wove into the elf's guard, wrapping an arm around him and slammed him head-first into the door.

Lakon spun on his heels, a gash across his forehead, forcing Min back with a slash. She yelped. A gash erupted from her chest to her shoulder. A glancing hit, but painful nonetheless. Lakon paused to laugh, and took another numbing draw from the inhaler. His eyes rolled back as the euphoria took hold.

He burst into action, flames roaring from his mouth.

Min caught his blade on hers and their swords locked. This was going to be an old school fight, a proper duel between two opponents.

They exchanged attacks with blinding speed. Arcs of black metal and silvery steel whistled through the air, clangs echoed through the forest. Min ducked under a swing. Lakon's attacks were wild and reckless, his superhuman speed and senses made up for his lack of discipline.

Min felt like she was fighting through water, slow and dumb compared to the elf. It was only her perfect form and well-drilled practice which overcame her short-comings. Each of Lakon's snapping, wild attacks were blocked with mechanical precision.

The blades locked.

Behind them, Trevor was wrestling with the one-handed wyrboar over the axe. He would have to fight this one himself.

Min pushed off on the elf's blade. His following attack almost took her head off. She slid away and bolted for the cover of the trees. Lakon pursued. The pair swerved through the forest, clashing in indecisive exchanges, sparks exploding between their weapons. Min felt her arms growing heavy, forearms burning as she tried to match the elf.

"You're getting tired, human!" cackled Lakon.

She dashed around a tree, expecting another attack, but there was no one. She froze, holding a low defensive stance.

Leaves rustled and Lakon burst into view from above. His weapon slammed into Min's and drove her against the trunk of a huge oak. "Weak!" he howled.

She grit her teeth. Sweat beaded across her brow. *Fuck*

you, pointy-eared freak. She slid her blade up his, hooking his hilt with her crossguard. She forced his blade out of the way and smashed the heel of her hand into his face.

The elf tumbled backwards; his black lips dripped blood. He licked his broken lip and smiled. "Oh, you are a fun one." He sprung back to his feet, howling as he resumed the attack with a barrage of overhead chops. He leapt into the air, his blade raised. She grunted, catching the blade on the edge of her sword. Blood seeped down from the gash on her chest, hot and sticky. Her arm trembled, threatening to buckle under the onslaught.

"You're nothing, human. You're a pest. Vermin." His hot breath reeked of rotten eggs. "I was here when this land was ruled by barrow lords! When the Earls dug for coal and when they left! I've seen generations pass but I'm still here! I am immortal! I am eternal!"

Min's arms trembled. He was stronger than his lithe frame should have allowed. She growled, holding him back.

"I'll be here long after NeoAnglia falls!" This aeflen fool believed he was a king in waiting. The gangster with a loose grip on reality and an addict to fume and power.

Nearby, Min saw the trees sway. A shadow was hurtling in their direction. Lakon didn't notice. He was too high and too excited by the fight.

Min grunted and kicked the elf in the stomach. He jumped back and landed daintily a few meters away. He grinned, feeling his victory was assured.

The crested theropod burst into view, its serrated jaws wide open. Lakon turned to see, but it was too late. The jaws clapped over the elf's chest, sinking dagger teeth into his flesh. Bright red blood hit Min's face.

She rolled out of the way and back to her feet. She ran. The screaming was finally silenced by a wet crunch.

♦

Min arrived back at the road. Three bodies lay on the gravel, the dead Marklander, the wyrboar, axe planted into the side of his thick skull, and Trevor.

NO. Min slid on the gravel to Trevor's side. He was bleeding from his side—a puncture wound, likely from the wyrboar's tusk. "Hey! Hey!" said Min. "Hey! Wake up!" She shook him until his eyes opened. He gasped, clutching his side. His shirt was stained red.

"Hi," he rasped. "Oh…that really hurts."

"Hey," she pulled up his shirt. "Yeah. Keep pressure. Stay awake."

Using her knife, she cut pieces of cloth from the clothes of the dead thugs and took one of their belts. Then she went to the vehicle to search for something to sanitize the wound.

Trevor croaked, "The glove box." He breathed slowly. "I got him…I actually got him."

"Yes, you did." She slid across the console. On the dash were a few pictures: Trevor with his family, Trevor with friends, Trevor close to a girl. Min grabbed all of those too.

Inside the glove box and console there were empty mickeys of liquor. She looked back at Trevor and held up a bottle of over-the-counter pills.

"Were you really going to check on your mother?"

"I…I don't know," he said. "Maybe not…"

Min ran back and began wrapping his wound, using the whiskey to sterilize and the cloth and belt to stop the bleeding. He looked up at her. "I guess I accepted Exposure pretty easy…"

"Yeah, far easier than I did."

She gave him the rest of the whiskey. He drained it in two gulps. She looked at him, saw the pain in his eyes.

"You keep calling this the Wrong Side. But maybe this world is for the best…a chance to start over…."

"It isn't."

"You don't know me, or what I've done, or what's been done to me."

"No," said Min. "But this side takes everything and gives nothing back. It's built that way. Here, we're cursed."

"I was already cursed."

Min frowned. *Maybe I just never thought about it that way.* She took his arm and helped him slowly to his feet. "Come on. Pak will patch you up."

They gathered what they could and began the long walk back to Penn Valley.

Min's Exposure had been devastating. Her life had been destroyed. She had lost everything, and in the most painful ways imaginable. But maybe, for Trevor and others like him, the Wrong Side was a new opportunity, a chance to start over, like he had said. A new world unshackled from the old.

Trevor grunted as blood seeped through the tourniquet. Each step took great effort on his part, but they had to make it. They had to hurry.

"You never answered," said Trevor as they ascended the slope, "is Min your real name?"

"Of course not."

Trevor looked at her. "Do you even know your real name?"

"No. I don't." She helped him over a log. "A lot of people lose their names at Exposure. Most pick new names, become a new person for this new world. Like they never existed on the Other Side in the first place."

"Or maybe this really is a dream? One we never wake up from?"

"Never."

She hauled Trevor through the forest, keeping him awake and keeping him alive. He had a chance for a better life now. A better life with Pak in Penn Valley or somewhere beyond these vile gang towns.

It was more than Min had after her Exposure. She had been left for dead, another body in a massacre. She had been saved by strangers, the monks of Chateau de Jean, but among them she had been an outsider. Trevor had a chance now. A chance for more than he had before. He could build something with Pak.

All she had to do was keep him alive until they reached Pak's workshop. In a world so very wrong, it was the one right thing she could do.

◆

The sun was still hidden behind the distant hills, the sky a black-purple haze. Trevor was resting, asleep on the couch, having been stitched up by Pak when they had returned. The gremlin had been worried sick. The kid would be alright, the shock of the fight and his first kill was a lot worse than the physical damage.

Min had waited for Trevor to fall asleep before she started packing her meager belongings. She shoveled some spare foodstuffs and supplies into a rucksack.

Pak sat on the coffee table, watching over the kid. "He's going to stay with me," whispered Pak. "He knows his stuff. He'll do well with me."

"I know," said Min, grabbing her weapon belt. She did up the buckle, adjusted the weight, and slowly realized it would be the last time she would walk out that door. She pulled the belt tight.

"You don't have to go, you know. You can stay." Pak's inhuman gaze met hers, bulbous blue eyes glistening. "You can find a new home with us."

Min grit her teeth. "Where's my money, gremlin?"

Pak's narrow shoulders sank and he got off the table. "You're a real bitch sometimes."

It's only been a few weeks, she told herself. *Why did I let myself become so attached?* "Save me the speech and give me my money."

"Fine. Fine. Fine." He reached into his pocket and pulled out a wad of cash. His spidery fingers began thumbing through the mixed bills. He did it slowly, methodically, as if taking his time would change her mind. Min snatched it, took a portion, and slapped the rest back on the desk.

"Crazy fucking human," sneered Pak.

"You know I have to leave."

"You don't have to!" hissed Pak, "You crazy bitch. We can help you. We can get out tonight; we can help you find what you're looking for."

"What I'm looking for isn't something I want to share. It's something I have to do alone."

Now Pak looked truly hurt. "No, it isn't. There's no good reason for that. We can help you!"

Min turned toward the door, refusing to look at his pleading face. Any longer and her resolve might break. "Go to Dunwich, tonight," she said coldly, "before Luka realizes what's happened. You'll both be better off in the cities."

"You—"

The barred door clanged behind her. *I can't let them come with me. I can't let anyone else get hurt.* Her hunt for the men who Exposed her was dangerous and uncertain. She couldn't live with herself if anyone else she cared about got hurt. *I've lost enough.* She vanished into the dark, crime-infested alleys of Penn Valley, onward on her journey.

A SOULLESS VISITOR

Another storm raged outside, completely ignored. The bed creaked with the enthusiasm of a long-imagined coupling. Hugo and Emmeline had spent the year flirting and joking, but had always avoided being alone with one another. They had had their studies to focus on and neither wanted to admit what they'd been feeling.

Then, with final exams over, they were finally left alone. And alone they finally acted on their mutual attraction.

Hugo had his arm around her, his brown hair clinging to his brow. Emmeline's naked flesh felt hot against his, her ash black hair lay in a tangled mess on the pillow. She smelled of perfume and smoke.

Their eyes met, and he kissed her, tasting her lips.

She smiled. "Well, it's taken you long enough to make a move."

"I was waiting for you to. I wanted to be sure—"

She kissed him hard. "Are you sure now?"

"Yes."

Emmeline's apartment was at the conical peak of the tower in the Collegiate of Light, one of the secondary institutions for the study of magic in Franco. Her room was a circular chamber of stone walls and hardwood floors. Against the walls stood a four-poster bed, a bureau, a chifforobe, and numerous packed bookshelves.

Hugo and Emmeline were ranked as Savants, esteemed among their fellow magicians.

"Here's a question," asked Hugo. Emmeline looked up, a delicate eyebrow raised. "If I left this place, would you come with me?"

"You want to leave?"

"I've wanted to leave for a long time. Ever since helping the Grand Master with his experiments."

Her grimace told him all he needed to know. The Grand Master, along with all the Masters of the Collegiate of Light, were conducting experiments in the depths of the castle, in the deepest dungeons. They had done things that kept Hugo up at night. Apprehensive with their powers, they conducted the same spells and rituals over and over again. Repeating the same nightmares and failures like it was an exercise in insanity.

"This place is sick," he whispered.

"Maybe," she said, resting her head on his chest. "We do what we can for science."

"We're magicians."

"We're scientists," she affirmed. "We simply study things the world doesn't understand. We study the preternatural so it may become the natural. You've said so yourself in your lectures."

"I know," he said, "but the Masters…they're just so self-absorbed, so stubborn... and they never listen. They stifle the growth we could have. They elevate only those who are as timid and corrupt as they are."

"Oh, my sweet," she cooed. "You'll advance to Magicien in due time. Talk to Master Leroux. He'll understand." She saw right through him, cutting right to the crux of his frustration with the Collegiate of Light. Maybe that was why he was so infatuated with her. She saw so clearly.

Emmeline leaned over the edge of the bed and took a pack of cigarettes from her clothes on the floor. She put a cigarette between her teeth. Hugo held up a finger. With a wordless incantation, he felt his hand go ice cold and a tongue of flame extended from his nail. He lit the tip of the cigarette.

"Thanks," she said, blowing smoke out of her nose. "I'm not ready to leave. I want to get a good contract with a family."

"That's what I mean," said Hugo, flicking the flame away and working the feeling back into his finger. "It all leads back to serving the families, the houses, the crown. It all leads to the courts of the nobility."

"Now you sound like a republican."

Hugo grimaced. "No, just tired of it all. I wish it could be about the science, the magic—"

His phone buzzed from within his pile of clothes on the floor. *Who the fuck...?* It was after midnight.

"Hugo!" shrieked a voice. He winced. It was Antoni Dumont, one of the Avanceé, a rank just beneath Savant. "We need you down here! Come to the Opposuitque Chamber, now!"

"What the fuck did you do?"

"We don't know! Come help us!"

Hugo looked at Emmeline, balled up on her side of the bed with the cigarette between her fingers. He gritted his teeth. "I'll be right down."

He got up and got dressed.

"What is it?" she asked.

"I don't know, but if they've fucked up the Opposuitque, the Masters will string them up."

She nodded. "I'll be here."

"Thank you." He leaned down and gave her one final kiss.

◆

Lightning flashed outside and thunder shook the castle.

Hugo hurried through a windowed gallery. The sprawling complex was a labyrinth that dated to the earliest arrivals on the continent. The stone walls glistened with condensation, gothic buttresses and spires outside sending long shadows across the landscape. Hugo could see the Laurentide Mountains spread out in the distance, peaks carpeted with patches of forest and rough Kanadian rock.

Collégiale de le Lumiée—The Collegiate of Light— was one of the isolated magical institutions of western Franco. All magic schools were under the direct purview of the King's Court and all magicians were registered with the state. Here, however, away from the capital and any urban centers, they could train and research in private.

Hugo turned down a spiral staircase at the end of the gallery. As a Savant, he was well on his way to becoming a fully inducted magician—a Magicien. He had been born in a rural Seigneurial village, had shown his magical abilities at an early age, and was taken to the Collegiate when he was eleven-years-old

Soon. Soon I'll be able to leave and they won't be able to stop me, he thought to himself.

He entered another windowed gallery, reaching the wing where the Opposuitque was housed. The storm wailed outside. Wind and rain lashed at the wizard spires. Lightning webbed across the sky. A bolt of electricity struck a distant tower. A lightning rod caught the bolt, but it shouldn't have needed to; the Collegiate had a barrier against such things. Magic was required to be kept bubbled within the castle to ensure no infection penetrated into the countryside, and to keep prying eyes and magical interference out. The Opposuitque took care of all of that.

What did those idiots do? Hugo quickened his pace, his shoes slapping against stone, unwilling to imagine the consequences if the barrier failed. His annoyance compounded into full blown rage. He didn't have time for this. He had better things to do. He turned a corner towards the Opposuitque chamber.

What the young magician did not see was the hunched

shadow that rose from the nearby crags of rock below the castle.

♦

Hugo swung open a pair of silver embossed doors. He shuddered; the fractured magic tingled every fiber of his being, lashing at his senses lashed with ribbons of broken energy. He held up his hands, momentarily blinded by the uncontrolled power.

Three robed acolytes stood at computer consoles. In the center of the chamber was a glass orb. A filament of lightning that should have been stable thrashed violently against the barrier. The glass was cracking, a single line of silver in the orb.

"What the hell did you do?" screamed Hugo.

Avanceé Antoni Dumont, the last son of a border Marquis, screamed something incomprehensible. He hammered at the controls, trying to get control of the situation.

Magic energy lashed the wall in a ribbon of blue and white light.

The castle was built on the confluence of major silver reserves and lay lines. The collegiate was a beacon of otherworldly power, which was why they needed the barrier.

That fucking idiot.

"What the fuck did you do?" screamed Hugo. He shoved Antoni aside, his eyes dashing over the console. *Polarity reversed,* he concluded. *Containment at critical.* "You fucking moron!" Hugo's hands danced over the console, adjusting settings, setting the polarity right.

He reached for the wand in his pocket but another lash of pure energy splintered the device and splashed against the walls. *Too late for wands.* Hugo gritted his teeth. *It's beyond what the device can handle.* He shut down the system, taking the machine's control of the energy away and relying entirely on his own powers. He threw up his hands, his eyes blazing bright blue as he connected to the wild magic. He reached out with his mind, wrenching the energy back into form. It was like grasping a ribbon in a blizzard. The power sent painful shivers up his arms. He screamed, grasping the fractured energy and forcing it back into the bottle.

The room went quiet.

The magic calmed. Hugo slammed his fist on a button and the entire system rebooted at a much lower level. The glass orb would need to be replaced before the barrier could return to full power.

Hugo fell to his knees, trembling. His hands hissed with steam. Pale burns splotched his skin. Magesblyte. He had touched the magic too aggressively. This was the cost. It was like if a mortal wrestled fire with their bare hands. Pain stung from his wrists to his fingertips.

"What. The fuck. Did you do?" said Hugo.

"W-we…" Antoni stuttered. He looked to the others for help.

The other two acolytes were Sasha Maros and Clair Gladwin. Aspirants—the lowest rank in the Collegiate. Both young women had fled NeoAnglia, a country where their connection to magic would likely have led to being burnt as witches. Sasha was Black with a bundle of braids, her family—bankers or peddlers of some note—sent her away to escape persecution. Clair was the blonde bastard daughter of a country Earl.

"We fucked up," said Sasha, stepping forward. She kneeled to tend to Hugo's hands with a medical kit. "We were testing a theory. We thought we could isolate a section of the barrier to block more than just the electro-magnetic spectrum. There was a paper from the Underground that argued a full protective shield could be made."

Hugo blinked. "And you thought tampering with the castle barrier was a good place to start?"

"We made a mistake."

"Was this theory even brought to the Masters?"

"They rejected it," said Clair, on the edge of tears. "We…we wanted to prove them wrong."

"You're all idiots," he hissed. The three junior wizards looked hurt, humiliated, and a bit terrified. "I will be telling the Masters in the morning."

Antoni and Clair looked like they'd been slapped. Sasha sighed, as though she had expected this consequence.

Hugo stood back up, rubbing his injured hands. "Now get this place cleaned up. Good night."

♦

Hugo walked back through the castle. The storm's battering of the castle had subsided, but he could still see distant flashes of lightning. The barrier was back up, a shimmer that the rainwater phased through. Everything would be fine in the morning. The Masters would repair the damage. The leak of magical energy from the collegiate would be minimal.

He cast aside the worry and returned to thoughts of Emmeline. He was approaching her dormitory wing, when he felt a shudder of cold air. He looked up, hearing wind whistling through the halls.

Oh no. He sped through the gallery.

Glass crunched beneath his shoes as he reached the

shattered window. Cold water sprayed his face. Wind howled through the gaping hole, whipping at Hugo's robes. Below were the jagged precipices of the mountainside, the crags of the Laurentide Mountains to which the expansive Collegiate clung.

His first thought was that the storm had blown out the window, but as his eyes drifted down the gallery, that hope was shattered. Wet footprints and shards of glass trailed down the hallway, vanishing into the darkness of the castle.

Oh no. Oh god, no.

The icy fingers of fear took him. He ran back to find the others. As he ran, he checked his pocket for his wand—the length of ash could be drawn upon by his magic without burning his hands.

♦

Hugo had called Sasha and Clair to meet him back at the Opposuitque Chamber. Antoni hadn't answered his phone. The chamber was quiet. The orb of glass was cracked, but the lightning within was kept contained between its filaments.

"What is it?" asked Sasha.

"I think, due to your experiment," said Hugo, "that something may have penetrated the barrier."

Clair jabbered and pleaded excuses while Sasha closed her eyes for a moment, letting the information settle onto her shoulders.

"I'm going to wake the Masters," said Hugo.

"If you do, we'll be tossed out or worse," said Sasha. *Probably worse*, thought Hugo. "We need to find it and catch it, whatever it is. Maybe it's a mountain lion or even just a feral orc."

"We can't. We don't know what this is," said Hugo.

"Then let's find out," said Sasha. "You can tell the Masters about our experiment; we'll get the lash anyway. If it's just a beast or something, then we can handle it. They don't need to know. Come on, Hugo, give us that. Don't make it worse for us."

"You've made it worse for yourselves," he hissed, still rubbing his injured hands. He turned to leave. Clair blubbered into tears.

"Hey!" said Sasha. "Her and I, we don't have anywhere else to go! You may hate this place, but it's all we have. You still have a family."

Hugo looked back. He could see the pain behind her determination. Sasha put an arm around Clair. They'd been through a lot together, from what Hugo heard. The two young, Anglo-raised girls—both chased out of their country—had only had each other before they could speak Franco. They had only had each other to share in their fear. Sasha glared at Hugo, protective of Claire.

"Fuck. Fine," said Hugo, despite himself. "Central corridor. Now."

♦

The three of them ascended through several wings of the castle. The storm returned with a vengeance. Rain hammered the stone walls and iron-barred windows, thunder quaked the castle.

As they walked through the long corridors of the central wing, Sasha raised her lantern, casting long shadows across the chamber. In the skeletal rafters above, the statue of a huge winged griffon watched. The storm had taken all warmth and familiarity from this place. An ever-intensifying dread hung over every buttress and passage.

"Come on," said Hugo. "If it's an animal, we can handle it. Anything else, I'm going straight for the Masters. Got it?"

Sasha nodded and sat down, setting the lantern in the exact center of the corridor. Clair stopped biting her thumbnail and sat down too. The three of them joined hands.

No-one said a word. One of the primary pillars of

understanding magic was simply listening, learning to feel the tendrils of magic in the air. All things gave off this force. It was the task of magicians to learn how to listen.

Hugo reached out with his consciousness. He felt wild, frustrated, and distracted. He wanted to return to Emmeline, but she would be asleep by now. He'd have to explain everything in the morning—

Focus.

He reached out, stretching his mind through the castle. Restraint and discipline, that was what made a wizard. The problem was the most cautious magicians lived the longest, leaving the Masters a gaggle of cowards—

Focus.

Hugo shackled the fraying ribbons of sensation and emotion into precise avenues for his mind to search. His emotions reached out, holding to the task as he searched for the intruder. He felt the others doing the same.

Sasha was powerful—more powerful than Hugo expected—but more importantly, she was disciplined. Her consciousness retrained the power into deliberate tracks, feeling out into the wings of the castle like searching fingers. Clair, on the other hand, was wild. Her fear made her senses weak and discordant. If she couldn't learn to control her emotions, she would make a poor magician.

The three searched the castle through their connections to the winds of magic.

Hugo reached through the upper spires, into the astrocons, cycloscopes, and orreries. Those who remained in the castle were asleep.

For a moment he was distracted by a scraping sound in the aether. He reached, following the sound. He came to an upper rafter and then to a spider web. He moved closer. A single fly had been caught in the lines of the web. The spider's mandibles plunged into the fly's thorax, keratin scraping. There was a soft slurping as the spider drank its prey's liquid entrails. The spider's soulless black eyes seemed to gleam with pleasure.

Hugo left the creature to its feast.

He searched through the empty apartments, labs, and fabricator workshops, then deeper down into the dungeons where the inmates were kept. The surrounding villages sent all their worst criminals here, saving the townsfolk the effort of having to execute them. His memories bled into his search, creating ghosts of his own as he checked each cell with his mind's eye. The horrors Hugo had witnessed in the Master's experiments haunted him in his nightmares. The screams clung to the walls like a fungus. The ghosts of their subjects would not sleep soundly unless expelled.

Hugo wrestled his focus back to the task and found

nothing. He searched for something out of place, something wrong, something that—

A high-pitched scream brought Hugo back to his body.

Clair was curled up on the ground, her head in her hands. She blabbered gibberish. Sasha was trying to calm her down.

"Clair," said Sasha. "Clair! What is it? Clair?"

"Hollow. Dead. Empty," she whimpered. "Empty. Empty. Em—"

"Clair!" said Sasha. "Focus. What did you see?"

The girl sniffed, rubbing her nose. "It's dead. It's hollow. It's nothing. It's nothing!"

"Where is it? Clair, where is it?" asked Sasha. "Breathe."

Clair slowly managed to get ahold of herself. She wiped her face. "Lecture Hall 18."

"That's between us and the Master's wing," said Hugo.

"We have to check," said Sasha.

"We don't know what we are getting into," said Hugo.

"I know we are trying to save our asses," said Sasha, hauling Clair to her feet. "Come on."

♦

They entered the lecture hall. The beam of Sasha's lantern glimmered off polished oaken desks. Hugo had his wand outstretched, a low glow lit the tip like a dying coal. A lectern sat atop a stage in front of a wall-to-ceiling chalkboard covered with complex formulas and lines script. It would look like the ramblings of a madman to the uninitiated.

Hugo and Sasha searched the darkened classroom, ducking under desks. Sasha cast her lantern light through the tiers of chair legs. Clair waited by the door, chewing her thumbnail. Hugo and Sasha had both tried reaching out to detect the presence the girl had felt, but felt nothing.

Hugo checked under a desk and in the back corner. He exhaled. "There's nothing."

Sasha circled a desk, rechecking a spot they had already searched twice.

"This is getting ridiculous," said Hugo. "I haven't felt anything. You haven't. We need to wake the Masters."

"Not yet," said Sasha.

Hugo walked toward Sasha, whispering so Clair couldn't hear him. "If it really was dangerous, we would have felt something." He shot a glance at Clair, who paced by the door, continuing to chew her thumbnail. "I know you two are close, but the experiment and the storm could be messing with her powers. It could have been nothing."

"And you want to wake the Masters over nothing?" said Sasha, eyes narrowed. "The Grand Master will—"

"I want to wake them over your experiment that compromised the barrier."

"Where's your pride? What happened to the Hugo who wanted to prove himself during Leroux's examinations?"

Her jabs at his pride wouldn't save her here. It was a poor tactic. She was baiting him and they both knew it. Her desperation to stay here was becoming apparent. *Can I really blame them?* Both of them had fled their country, escaping mobs and fanaticism. Hugo pushed aside his frustration. "You really want to dig yourself into this pit? We're going to Master Leroux. He's understanding at the best of times. Fair?"

Sasha glared.

"Guys…" said Clair.

"You may think he's fair," said Sasha, ignoring her. "But not to us, not to foreign witches. You're a star pupil, he loves you. You just can't see it."

Hugo scoffed. *Another reason to leave this place,* he thought. *This place is sick.* It had been sick for a long time. The cowardly, cautious masters, indulgent and corrupt.

The darkness here was far worse than any monster from the mountains. Hugo needed to leave this place—

"Guys!" cried Clair.

"What?" said Hugo.

They could see Clair was trembling, on the verge of a hysterical attack. She gripped the door frame to hold herself up. Blood dripped onto the floor from above. Sasha slowly cast the light upward. Hugo gasped.

Sasha dropped her lantern. She ducked behind the desk and vomited on the floor. Hugo was frozen, hands trembling. He steadied himself on a chair as his legs threatened to buckle beneath him. No. No. It wasn't possible. Something like this couldn't happen here. It wasn't possible.

Hanging from the ceiling was Antoni. Or what was left of him. His arms hung limp past his head, his robes stained with his own blood. He was split down the back with his spinal column ripped open and dripping fluids. His face was pale, eyes wide and vacant. Blood dripped from his fingers to the floor. He looked like a pig carcass set to drain in a butcher shop.

Whatever had entered the castle was no mountain creature or wild abhuman.

Clair screamed, falling to her knees. She crawled out to the hallway. "Hollow. Dead. Empty. It's nothing. Hollow.

Dead. Empty. It's nothing."

It hadn't been the experiment that wrecked Clair's sight. Her wild emotionality was the only thing that could detect this creature, whatever it was. A null, soulless thing, this beast, this wizard killer. It wasn't something Hugo could understand—that's what scared him the most. His studies, skills, rank of Savant, striving for Magicien...none of it could help him now.

Like a child crying for their parent, he whimpered, "Now we need the Masters."

♦

They rushed up to the Master's wing, Sasha half-carrying Clair. Around and around, they climbed the spiral staircase. Hugo almost slipped when they passed a tapestry that had been slashed in half. They continued around and around until they arrived at Master Leroux's apartment.

Leroux, a master pyromancer who taught practical magic, was a veteran of several feudal wars. He kept his classes as ordered and disciplined as a military squad. He was tough, but fair.

He had stood over Hugo during his first year and handed him a blade of grass to transfigure. Leroux had called Hugo, "Aspirant." He never used anyone's name until they reached Savant. He was the one Master that Hugo respected.

Hugo froze. He gripped his wand with white-knuckled terror.

The door was broken open, leaning on its hinges. Hugo cast his lantern light through the portal. The desk and bed were overturned. Streaks of blood dragged from the bed. Hugo followed the trail up to the rafters.

Master Leroux hung from the ceiling, blood dripping down his muscled arms. His back was ripped open, ribs jutting out from eviscerated flesh, his spinal column exposed, a hole at the nape of his neck.

Clair fell against the wall, curling up on a step, sobbing.

Sasha looked sick again, but she shook herself free. "Come on, Hugo! Come on! We need the Grand Master!"

Hugo allowed himself to be pulled away.

♦

They ran to the main wing of the Collegiate, to the grand halls where many of their classes, rituals, and experiments took place.

Hugo couldn't put the sights he had just seen out of his mind.

Why string them up? Why remove the spines? Why take the brains? *What kind of creature did this?* It was too specific, too planned. It wasn't the feasting of a hungry beast, but the calculated acts of a creature with intent. A tactical planner. A beast with a purpose.

They followed the spiral staircase until they reached a hallway to the Grand Master's chambers. Hugo threw open the door, then screamed.

The apartment of the Grand Master's adepts was ransacked. Their bunks were bathed with blood. Four bodies lay face down, their backs ripped open like torn packages. Their spines had been exposed and drained with furious brutality.

Sasha ran through the room to the Grand Master's quarters. Hugo followed. They threw back the iron barred door. The apartment was destroyed like the other rooms, desk and shelves shattered. Hugo saw the old man propped against the upturned bed, clutching at a huge gash on his chest with terror in his eyes..

A huge, hairy silhouette turned and hissed at the interruption. With blinding speed it dove out through a stained glass window, too fast to get a clear picture of. The noise and cold of the storm filled the chamber.

Hugo slid down next to the old man. He had the white beard and watery blue eyes one expected of an old wizard.

Hugo tried to stop the bleeding. He was no healer. The old man clutched Hugo's robes, his eyes watering. "It's from us," croaked the old man, blood seeping from his skull. "The experiments. What did you do with the failures?"

Hugo gulped. "I—I followed your orders. I disposed of them."

The dying man clutched Hugo's sleeve. His eyes pleaded. "Where?"

The answer clung to Hugo's throat. "The sewage outflow… below the dungeons…"

"Then it's you who has doomed us…" They were Grand Master Falco's final words. The man went limp, the blood loss and damage far too much for the old magician.

Hugo rose. "Find everyone else and get them out. They need to know."

He looked at Sasha; she stood by the broken window that overlooked the sprawling castle complex. Hugo went to stand next to her. Through the opening, he saw a hunched shadow clinging to the side of a distant wing of the castle. It crawled along the walls with rapid insectoid movements, its back a matt of black hair. Its vaguely human form had a sickly white complexion and unnaturally elongated limbs splashed with crimson. Around its waist was a leather skirt. It had a huge blade strapped to its back; a rusted longsword far longer and thinner than any weapon of its size should have been.

It was climbing toward the dormitories.

"There's no hope," said Sasha. "We have to get out of here! We have to evacuate."

"Go! You two get everyone out," said Hugo. His panic drove him mindlessly toward the door. "Get a message to Duc Leopold. Get a message to the Capital. Tell them that the Collegiate has fallen. They need to know!"

All our secrets. All our work. Wasted.

He ran through the castle. Legs pumping, he skidded on his shoes at each corner. He came to a gallery

Hugo gasped in horror.

Through another window, he saw the creature climbing a distant spire. It was climbing toward Emmeline.

Hugo hurried toward the dormitories. He drew his wand from within his robes.

◆

Hugo shouldered a door open. His face dripped in sweat; his lungs burned. He had been screaming for Emmeline the entire way up the tower, desperately trying to reach out with his telepathic magic.

Everything was blank.

Numb.

It was as if the magic that pervaded the castle had been sucked away, turning the building to a lifeless crypt. Hugo screamed and hammered at every door he passed. "Evacuate! Evacuate! This is not a drill!"

"Where are the Masters?" groaned one acolyte, rubbing her eyes.

"Dead! Run to the south entrance! Get to the village! Run!"

He heard a scream come from up above. It was Emmeline.

Hugo burst into her apartment, his face twisted, pained, and disgusted.

The desk was knocked over. The window was broken inward, now a portal to the raging storm outside. The iron bars were gnarled like broken twigs. The single lamp on her desk cast light upward into the rafters.

Emmeline was slumped face down on the bed, unmoving.

Hugo's stomach dropped. His heart wrenched; he was unable to see if she was alive or not. *We didn't even have our chance.* He looked up at the creature leering over her. Hugo's throat filled with bile.

The creature rose higher on its legs, filling the chamber with its immensity.

A huge mane of black hair grew from its head and down its back. Its face had once been human, but was now mutated into a wolfish monstrosity. Its canines were as long as sabres; blood streamed down its cracked lips.

The beast unslung it's too-long and too-thin blade. The hilt was made of a thorny black metal that looked like ivy. The monster's unnaturally long fingers clutched the weapon with delicate grace.

Hugo felt then what Clair had been screaming about. *Hollow. Dead. Empty.* He felt it all around him, crushing him, a suffocating nothingness. His connection to magic was being throttled by this unliving monster.

The wolfish face held a pair of deep, hollowed sockets. It let out a hot, sickly breath, a hungry rasp for sustenance. Hugo looked into its eyes. He knew it, as he ought to.

He had been the one who cast it out.

Experiments fail. Sometimes you have to make the hard choice to remove the failures. The Masters had ordered Hugo to cast a body away. The monster had been one of the nameless criminals left to the Masters. It had been genetically modified using magic, an alchemical attempt to manipulate life, a new type of arcane science. They thought the body had failed and died on the operation table.

Hugo's mind rushed to grasp at possibilities. *How?* His scientific mind, unable to comprehend the loss of Emmeline, grasped for a hypothesis. It could have grown in the crevasses below the castle, feeding on the runoff and leavings of the Collegiate. It was a starved creature that lived off of magical sewage, a junkie for the primordial powers—the interdimensional energies and forces which bound all things in existence. The experiments could have warped a man's biology to crave such things.

It would have been watching from the peaks, waiting and plotting until the barrier faltered, revealing the beacon of magical powers.

Now it had come home.

It craved the most magically rich substance imaginable: the spinal fluid of wizards.

Hugo raised his wand with a trembling hand.

The creature burst from its position, its jagged sword swinging.

Hugo screamed and charged.

SHIPWRECK AT NORWICH

Heavy waves crashed against the shore. Liz walked along the pebbled trail, her boots crunching as she stepped on the small stones. The rain fell in sheets that slammed into her, sending icy shivers through her body. Though the path she traveled was flanked by trees, the tall birches and spruces offered little protection against the Atlantic winds.

She clutched her cloak closer, trembling with cold, irritated she'd been caught in the springtime storms that plagued the coast.

Soon, through the lashes of silver rain, the lights of a town came into view.

Her stomach growled. "Soon baby, soon. We're almost there," she said, and continued down the path until she came to the cobblestone road.

She passed into the town, holding herself against the wind that whistled through the alleys. The brick walls and pointed tar roofs squeezed around the solitary figure. Lightning cracked, briefly illuminating the keep that overlooked the town.

Two trucks were parked along the road—rickety peddler vehicles, stocked with pots, pans, and dozens of other wares for sale; things impossible for people in small towns and villages to produce. Two apprentice peddlers stood under an awning near the vehicles, smoking, watching Liz approach.

Up ahead she could see the sign of an inn swaying on its hinge. *Kraken End.* The stranger, Liz, hurried passed the apprentices toward the inn that promised warmth, rest and safety.

The inn's door swung open and slammed shut, quieting the howl of winds and rain outside. Liz stood in the entrance. She was soaked to the core; her feet sloshed in her boots and her cloak weighed a metric ton. She was freezing, tired and hungry.

All chatter in the common room ceased as the inn's handful of patrons turned to stare at the stranger. Robert Johnson's "Me and the Devil Blues" crackled from a run-down jukebox. Liz glared back at the townsfolk, and they quickly returned to their drinks and conversations. The hum of the inn returned, and the scratchy twang of the guitar through the juke with it. The walls were plastered with seaside memorabilia: anchors, flags, nets, pictures of crews, and prized fishing trophies. A fire crackled in a stone fireplace, radiating warmth throughout the inn.

"Hey!" barked a voice. "You're dripping on mah' floor! Buy a drink or get out!"

A middle-aged Anglo woman stood a few tables away, a tray of foaming drinks in her hands.

"Beer. A big beer."

"Spot by the fire." The woman snarled. "Let it all hang by the fire. Got money?"

Liz nodded and crossed over to the fireplace. She peeled off her cloak, her flannel, her boots, and her socks, setting them all by the fire. Her bag thunked against the floor, and she placed her weapon belt on the armrest of a massive red chair before sinking into its cushion, her body aching from the day's traveling.

Above the mantelpiece were a trio of plaques with huge black beaks like those of parrots, but sharper. The biggest of them was serrated. The stranger stared up at them. Trophies. Taken from the krakens slain along the NeoAnglian coast.

The patrons of the inn appeared to be local fishermen,

dock workers, peddlers, and the like, all rugged, white Anglos with wind burnt faces and calloused hands.

A peddler approached her. His purple coat was ragged and his long unkempt grey hair stuck out around his ears. He hunched over under his oversized backpack stuffed with wares and supplies. Toolss, bags of medical supplies, and other luxuries from the modern world hung from D-rings on the sides of his bag. His blue eyes smiled down at her.

"Good evening, miss! How are ya? Can I interest ya in my wares?"

She knew there wouldn't be many more chances to stock up on basic supplies. She leaned in close, what little remained of her disposable cash in hand. "How many lady products can I get for this?"

The older man smiled; several of his teeth were missing. He discretely held up a box of tampons and a bundle of condoms wrapped in an elastic band. "One or the other miss? Neither by the bit."

"Come on," said the stranger. "Give me three condoms and the box."

"Nah, miss," said the peddler. "These are hard to come by. Lucky I had 'em at all. Folks don't buy them in pieces. Don't trust 'em then."

A side door opened, interrupting their conversation,

and a young man returned to his seat across the common area. He was an Asian man with a strong, handsome face; he appeared to be in his late twenties. *At least six years younger than me for sure*, thought Liz. He smiled at the stranger before returning a tattered paperback book. *The House on the Borderland* by William Hope Hodgson. He pulled a cigarette from a box with his mouth as he read.

"Give me the goddamn condoms." They had other uses in the wilds.

The older man snickered as he handed the pack over. "Excellent choice, my lady. Thoughtful. I don't recommend staying long enough to use 'em here. I'm leaving with the convoy. You should too."

Liz's stomach growled. "Why's that?"

"This town—it's cursed, miss!" he checked over his shoulder, making sure no one could hear him, and whispered, "Cursed. Damn place is better left alone. Get out while you can."

He moved on, leaving Liz to herself. She tapped her finger, looking around the inn. Its guests all seemed as relaxed as they could be, given the storm. *Old man is overreacting.* She glanced back at the younger man. His eyes darted back to his book. The promise of warmth and company was too good to pass up. It was too cold out there.

The stranger got up and crossed over to the traveller. "Might I trouble you for a smoke?"

"Of course, my lady."

Liz took a RedRoll from the box and allowed the man to light it with a boxy chrome lighter. Their equally dark brown eyes met. She took a long draw and let the smoke leak through her nose. "Thank you," she said with a wink.

She returned to her chair and, with her feet up, enjoyed the cigarette alone.

The fire crackled, sending sparks up the chimney. Flames danced in tendrils as they burnt away the logs. She watched the flames, and her mind drifted into unfortunate and unwanted memories; not awake enough to keep away from the images, the screams, the gunshots, the screech of a crashing vehicle. Falling into a waking dream, she saw a bus burning along a road, ribbons of flame climbing into the night sky. A man in a black cloak lifted a black-bladed sword. He smiled when he brought the blade down.

A squeal from the jukebox snapped Liz out of the nightmare. The owner, the large Anglo woman, slammed a fist against the box, setting it back on track. She set a huge, foaming mug of beer next to the stranger, her eyes cast down suspiciously. "Food?" She was carrying a tray.

"Yes, please."

"Suppose you'll be wantin' a bed. There isn't any."

The woman walked away before Liz could respond. *I'll have to figure something out*, she thought. She hadn't realized it, but she had sucked the cigarette to the filter. She flicked the butt into the fire. Her stomach was roaring for food now.

"Another went into it," said a voice. It was one of the fishermen at a nearby table.

Three men leaned over their tankards, their gaunt, wind-burnt faces covered in scraggly brown or grey hair. The stranger watched them in the corner of her vision, and she could tell by their postures they were scared.

"Who?"

"Martin Borson's daughter."

"No!" said the other.

"Last night," said the first fishermen.

"And nobody has gone after her?" protested the third. "No one stopped her?"

"No one knew," said the fisherman. "We need to burn that thing to the ground. It needs to be destroyed."

"It can't be," said the other. "Lord Nors knows it. He keeps calling Dunwich and they do nothing."

"Nothing, like always."

"Nothing," said the third. "God save the king and all his fucking earls." He raised a sarcastic toast to their overlords.

"Hush up," hissed the first fisherman. "You want to end up like the rebels?"

Liz stopped listening after that. The owner brought her a bowl of seafood chowder and a heel of bread. The stranger handed the owner the last of her money. She ate slowly, trying to savour the warmth. She needed to figure out how to get a place to stay without any money.

She glanced at the younger man, who smiled at her again.

This time she smiled back. She needed to get warm.

◆

By the time the storm calmed, the younger man was fast asleep. He had been eager and excited, performing admirably. He was warm and his breathing helped against the quiet. An eerie calm seemed to have a hold over the entire town. Liz sat up against the ornate headboard with a cigarette between her fingers, smoke trailing up past her head, her naked body half-covered by the sheet.

Sleep struggled to hold her. The nightmares were growing worse the further she fought her way south. Every time she closed her eyes she saw those cloaked swordsmen. *Will it ever end?* She wondered. *Or will I have to relive it every time I sleep until I collapse?*

She looked down at the necklace she usually kept hidden. A ring. A simple ring. She just couldn't remember who had worn it.

She got up, feeling restless, and went out onto the balcony.

The iron rail dripped with residual rainwater. Her bare feet were tickled by the icy cold puddles. With the cigarette hanging from her mouth, she looked over the town.

Crucifix-topped spires and iron-barred windows gave the seaside town a foreboding gloom. It was a dying town with abandoned buildings left to rot like corpses. It already seemed like a ghost town. The oil lamps flickered. The few remaining lights offered no warmth, only the promise of their eventual dying light. The wharf was coated in barnacles and salt. Fishing sloops and trawlers sloshed in their berths, bloated bodies waiting to sink in a storm.

At the apex of the settlement, on cliff's edge, sat the castle of House Nors; The roost of Lord Nors, the local aristocrat, the last of a dying house. The castle's single lighthouse tower and stone walls were broken, long battered and blasted by the Atlantic winds. The circling beam at the tower's crown was dim, flickering as though it, like the town, didn't have much time left. Liz flicked her cigarette away. Places like this had been dying a slow death for decades.

Beyond the fortress were the craggy cliff face that were shrouded in darkness…but there was something more. Something impaled on the rocks of the beach.

She meant to return to bed, but paused.

Her eyes narrowed.

Standing in the street below was a single solitary figure. A tall man in a cloak, sword in his hand. The faceless spectre looked up at the stranger.

She gasped, and her heart leaped into her throat. Full-body terror crept up from her icy-cold feet, to her spine, and into her brain. Heart drumming, palms hot, and eyes dilated, she stepped back, bumping into the doorframe.

She glanced back at the bed, seeing the lump of her sleeping lover. When she glanced back the spectre was gone.

Her mouth tasted fuzzy, like spoiled milk and electricity.

It's nothing. It's nothing. Just a ghost. A memory.

Uneasy, she went back to bed, struggling to get some rest.

◆

The black-cloaked figure stood over the woman with the flames roaring behind him. The night echoed with the screams of innocent civilians. The cloaked men cut them down as they ran. They were demons, predators, thirsty only for blood. The man raised his sword. His eyes sparkled with murderous contempt.

A woman screamed.

Liz opened her eyes, sitting up in bed. It was early, the light of dawn peeking in from the balcony. The younger man, she thought his name was Ian, was still asleep. She rubbed her eyes and smacked her lips, still tasting the strange sensation on her tongue. She gathered her clothes off the floor, her gear off a corner chair, and slunk out the door.

The common room was empty with the chairs on top of tables. The fireplace crackled with dying embers. The kraken beaks were somehow more disturbing than a mounted deer head. She slipped out of the inn, hoping to leave town once she gained a bit of cash.

The cobblestone roads of Norwich smelled of fish and rain. Men and women went about their daily activities, smoke rising from their RedRolls and tobacco pipes. Their windblown faces and downcast eyes offered no hope for the dying town. Ship bells echoed from the wharf as fishermen returned with meager catches.

Liz found herself at the edge of an awakening market square. The early catches of the day were set in ice trays. The farmers with sold boxes of onions, potatoes and dried herbs and their wives sold apples and in season vegetables. A butcher hammered down a cleaver, splitting a huge Atlantic bluefish in two. Another farmer hurried pygmy theropods to slaughter. They were like razor-sharp chickens covered in thin black and red proto-feathers. Their burbling chirps made a sailor curse and kick at the prehistoric, almost-avian creatures.

That metallic, rotten taste hadn't left Liz's tongue. She was hungry, but couldn't imagine keeping anything down.

She remained unsettled by the visions from the night. She gripped the hilt of her own sword to still her trembling hand. The fear crawled into her chest. *No,* she told herself. *He's dead. He's been dead for five years.*

She left the market and came to the local bulletin near the sheriff's office. Her eyes scanned the wanted posters and job offers. She needed money. There were reports of a bandit west of the town, but the poster was over six months old. The requests for experts in the mystic arts and help with wizardly matters were well outside Liz's purview. There was a request for a monster slayer, but that was a year out of date.

There were a *lot* of missing person notices. Men, women, boys, and girls—the disappearances didn't have a pattern. They seemed random and aimless. *Maybe there really is a curse?* There was certainly something wrong with the town. Liz smacked her lips. That alien taste just wouldn't leave her.

A pair of deputies leaned against the porch railing of the sheriff's office. They wore scavenged armored vests with belts that hung with revolvers and truncheons. They watched the stranger, hoping she would give them a distraction from their boredom. Liz moved on. *Nothing for me...*

As she wandered through the winding roads and alleys of the salt-stained town she considered her next move. With no money, what chance did she have out in the NeoAnglian countryside? She was alone.

Fucking hell, she cursed herself, *idiot*. She should have gone with the peddler convoy. They might have even paid her for the protection. Now she was stuck in this cursed town with no money and no opportunities. Between the wharfs' warehouses she saw the site the fishermen had discussed so ominously. Castle Nors, in all its inglorious disrepair, as sharp and unsettling as a rusted saw blade.

Below the castle was the dark mass she had spied during the night, a huge shipwreck impaled on the rocks.

It was an ugly carcass of salt blasted metal. Charcoal grey waves crested and slapped against the wreck. There was a huge gaping hole in its hull, like the toothy maw of a breaching shark. Its hollow darkness called to the woman. The fuzzy, rotten taste in her mouth grew more intense. Her vision became hazy and a whistle echoed in her ears. She took a step forward, feeling drawn to it.

The cloaked swordsman stepped out of the shadows; he took a long, faceless look in Liz's direction before walking into the shipwreck and disappearing once again.

She froze, staring at the black portal. She felt drawn to the wreck, as though someone was guiding her hand or calling her closer.

Shouting voices snapped her back to reality. Locals passed her by; a baker left his shop and two seamstresses ran towards the noise. Liz followed the growing crowd into a market courtyard. There were only a few stalls and many of the buildings were boarded up. The entire town felt like a graveyard with its dead still walking the avenues.

A suited herald stood on a platform flanked by a squad of riflemen. Liz glanced at the crowd, seeing anxious, terrified, and exhausted faces. They whispered and gossiped, trying to figure out what was happening. What news would their lord offer? Had word come from the capital? Was a representative from the king coming? Had there been an attack by Franco? Raids from Marklander pirates? A surge in kraken attacks? Any news was bad news...the question was, just how bad would it be?

"Good Anglofolk of Norwich, hear me, hear me," said the herald. "I bring troubling news. During the night's storm, another of our people vanished. Our Lord Alfred Nors's daughter, Lady Lilian Nors, has disappeared."

Shouts and whispers rippled throughout the crowd. The revelation that even their overlord wasn't immune to the curse troubled the townsfolk.

"Our Lord and Lady Nors are mourning the loss of their daughter; they will take no petitions for the day."

More shouts and whispers stirred throughout the crowd. One woman shouted, "What about our daughters? Our sons? Our lost folk?" Shouts of agreement followed. They were all mourning their missing families. "What about our people? What will Lord Nors do?"

The herald ignored the pleas and retired back to the safety of the castle.

Liz looked past the fortress again, seeing the shadows behind the curve of the cliffs. Her stomach churned with an irrational, feral, and nearly desperate need to know. That drive that made one slow down to see a car crash... to watch a wild animal feast...to see what made that sound upstairs… She needed to find out what was going on here. *Why is he here? Why can I see him?* He was dead. Why could she see him?

She turned and headed back to the inn, not knowing where else to start. Townsfolk moved out of her way. She was a vicious-looking mercenary with a black cloak and snarling wolves on the hilt of her sword.

They were as terrified of her as they were of the curse.

They just didn't know how scared she was.

♦

The common room of the inn was empty. *Thank god,* thought Liz. She didn't want to interact with Ian. She heard activity in the kitchen. When she entered, she found the woman from the previous night standing at a stove stirring a massive pot of chowder. Wondrous smells filled Liz's senses, fresh baked bread, roast apples, fried fish, and bacon.

The woman glanced up, one eyebrow raised. She was in her forties, heavy, pretty, her round face splashed with flour. Her brown hair touched with silver and apron splashed with grease.

"Well, you're brazen. Managed to find a bed, did ya? I admire the practicality," said the woman. "What can I do for ya?"

"Tell me," said Liz, ignoring the comments and picking a piece of bread from a tray. Hunger finally forcing her to act, she tore into the soft loaf. "Why is everything so fucked here? What the hell has been going on?"

"You're blunt."

"Answer me."

The woman stopped stirring. "You've seen something, haven't you?"

"Just answer the question."

"What's your name?"

Liz didn't respond, she was a stranger to this town and that was all she needed to be. Her narrow brown eyes watched intensely, waiting for the answer she wanted.

"Well, my name is Marsha Willkins," she set the oar-sized wooden spoon down. "I had three sons. One went to war in Franco and never came back. One is in school in Dunwich—bless him—and the third…Eddie. Edward, named after the king—bless him— vanished six months ago. Just disappeared, like God decided he didn't exist. Everyone around here has a story like that."

"Why?"

"You see the shipwreck? The one below the castle?"

Liz nodded, eating more fresh bread.

"About two years ago, it washed up on our shore. When the lord's men went in to investigate, they found nothing. A few days later, things started going wrong. The men went mad. Their screams went through the walls. It went on until they couldn't take it anymore. Bran Araskin walked into the water to get the sleep he wanted."

"Where did the ship come from?"

"It's a Dunwich ship."

"So, it's part of the Royal Navy?"

Marsha shrugged. "Lord Nors won't remove it. Says it would be betrayal if he touched it. Acts like he's doing a favour for the king,which I 'spose is true—bless him." She coughed. "But none of the king's men have come to salvage it yet."

Liz chewed the perfectly fluffy bread. Something was off.

"You just accept that? 'King is busy, Lord Nors is a good overseer.'" Her voice fluttered on the edge of shouting, contempt lacing her words.

Marsha glared, insulted. "Stranger with a sword comes in, calls us peasants. I see it in your eye. We do our duty. Good Anglofolk obey their king. We're no rebels. Rebels die here. The lords know what America has become. They listen to the words of Exposed folks. They keep us from falling to pieces."

It was a useless conversation. Any Anglo would say the same thing. They depended on their feudal world order to survive, and couldn't imagine anything else

"There's something more," said the stranger. "What does a royal shipwreck have to do with the disappearances?"

Marsha shuffled nervously. "Old man Teeg, before he vanished too, went inside. He said there was something in there, something he couldn't understand. Said something about his nightmares."

"What?"

The woman shrugged her wide shoulders.

The bread didn't taste right. That's what was wrong. It should have been satisfying, but it felt like chewing air.

"The curse?" asked Liz

Marsha met the stranger's eyes, giving a slight nod. There was terror in her eyes. The curse.

"You sure Lord Nors even sent his request to the capital?"

Marsha nodded.

"I don't believe you. His own daughter is gone now,

and still he hides in his castle and lets it continue."

Marsha looked away; she picked up her spoon and began stirring the chowder before it burned. "You should leave, miss. Just leave Norwich. Leave before it takes you too."

"Will do," said the stranger, leaving the half-eaten bread.

The hazy feeling on her tongue continued.

In due time. She ventured out into the streets, watching the comings and goings of the people as she wandered. She avoided the bus station when she saw Ian waiting in the shelter. He was leaving and right to do so.

Christ, why am I staying? Liz asked herself as she circled back towards Castle Nors. She could leave hungry and penniless, she had done it before. Why wait? Why indulge the morbid curiosity? She stood in a street below the castle, eyes looking up a fissure in the wall.

She had been searching NeoAnglia for rumours of the men with black-bladed swords...and now she was seeing a ghost of one. *Am I just insane?* No. Worse. She exhaled, and knew she couldn't leave until she found out what was going on. She had to face this ghost. She had to overcome the nightmares she had been cursed with for five years.

♦

Mists swirled across the cobblestone roads. Town deputies patrolled with oil lanterns. Over the dilapidated buildings the sky had fallen into a dark ashen grey. Liz walked back towards Castle Nors. Her boots sloshed in a puddle. The buildings leaned in around her. In the tall windows she saw surviving townsfolk watching, clutching crosses and talismans. Praying for the demons to go. Praying for the night of horrors to end. They hid within their crypt-like homes and clutched their children, waiting for their own turn to disappear.

She reached a broken rift in the castle. She had been watching the patrols all day, waiting for the right moment. Now her chance had come.

Her sword stowed on her back, hands wrapped with strands of cotton, her cowl hiding her face, she cut across the road at blinding speed before launching up the broken wall of the castle. Using cracks in the stone wall as handholds, she scaled up to the parapet. Hidden in the shadows of Norwich, she was invisible.

Sweat beaded across her brow as she climbed. Her Master would be proud of her, though he would never show it. She balled her fists inside a gap in the stones, creating an anchor to pull herself up even further. Movies always made this seem easy—nothing could be further from the truth. *Just bite down and bear it.* Her focus was only on the next step, not the pain she felt as she climbed.

Her fingers curled over the edge of the parapet, nails clawing at the rough stone. Her face rose up above the edge, scanning the walls for patrols. Two guards were about ten meters down the wall from her, huddled around a lantern and smoking.

The stranger vaulted onto the walls and slunk into Castle Nors, searching for the mourning lord and lady.

♦

The main hall of Castle Nors had fallen into the same decay as the rest of the town. The low ceiling, rough stone walls and oaken rafters all looked like they were ready to collapse at any moment. The banners were faded and torn. The remaining long table was set against a wall.

Liz saw the lone lord sitting in a chair near the fireplace. He stared into the flames, lost in their fluxing tendrils as well as his grief. He was a haunted little man, with a ruddy, round face, salt-and-pepper whiskers, and heavy bags under his dark eyes. He wore a simple, disheveled suit and his chin rested on his fist.

The stranger approached him, appearing like the ghost from her nightmare.

"Are you here to kill me?" he whispered without looking up.

"Why would I be?"

He glanced up, seeing the warrior woman in a black cloak, the hilt of her sword poking out from over her shoulder. His watery eyes studied her. "Because someone in town is paying you to."

"No."

"Then why are you here?"

"Why is that cursed shipwreck still on the beach?"

"Why do you care?"

She ignored the question. "Why do the ghosts haunt this place? Why do you let this continue?"

He blinked and smacked his lips. "You feel it? You taste it? It's in the air, in our water."

"What is it?"

"Magic."

Such a silly word, innocuous, from children's stories. Silence followed, pregnant and bloated, broken only by the crackle of the fire. The stranger smacked her lips, feeling the tingle of magic in the air. "Go on, old man."

"The RRS *Magellan*, a research vessel from the Misktatonic University, was on a return voyage from distant lands when it was hit by a hurricane."

"We don't know where the ship was returning from?"

"No. Only that it washed up on my shores. The messengers I sent to Dunwich have been ignored. I have begged for and demanded that the government send qualified experts, the king's scientists and magicians, but none have come. Miskatonic doesn't want anyone to know what they did."

"And *you've* just let this continue?"

"What would you have me do? My men won't touch it. I am left on my own. Whatever *Magellan* did on its voyage... Misktatonic buried it and I can see why."

"*You,* Lord Nors, are the ruler of this town. You could have found a way. Hauling it, burning it, anything. You let it sit and rot and hoped it would go away—"

"And now my daughter is gone because of it. I *did* try to remove it. I sent men to dispose of it and every single one was cursed with ghosts and nightmares. Accidents, broken arms—everything that could go wrong did. After that, neither my men nor the townsfolk would touch it; no one would obey my orders to go near that place. Our curse was complete."

She looked down at him and saw a weak man. To her, these were just excuses. He could have done more. *He blames his people for his missing daughter. They blame him for his failure.* The stranger was disgusted. "You've all just accepted your misery and done nothing about it. All of you. Pathetic, lord and peasants alike."

She marched away, understanding what she would have to do.

"What are you going to do?"

"I'm going to fix this." *Someone has to. Someone has to face the nightmares.*

He watched her leave out the servants' passage.

♦

The waves slapped against the pebbly beach as the winds whistled against the jagged cliffs. The shipwreck, an inglorious carcass of barnacle-covered metal, clung to the shoreline.

Liz stood on the beach, holding a torch taken from Castle Nors. She glanced at the town over her shoulder.s Mists swirled through its streets. The low glow of street lamps gave Norwich the quiet foreboding of a hospital waiting room.

Liz looked back at the wreck. She grimaced, her legs growing weak and threatening to go out from under her.

The ghost stood just outside the entrance.

Sharp boulders flanked the gaping hole in the ship's hull, making it look like a shark's mouth breaching the ocean. The cloaked swordsman stared at her, his face hidden within a black cowl. He turned and entered the opening, vanishing into the darkness.

Liz walked slowly, timidly, torch in hand.

The taste of electricity, rotten eggs, and moldy bread clung to her senses and sent shudders down her spine

I have to face him, she told herself. *I have to. He can't keep haunting me.* If she left the town, left this place to its death, she'd never be able to face the rest of them. She had to find them. How could she hope to face them if she couldn't face the wreck?

She breathed in, tightened her grip on the torch, and let out a slow exhale. She entered the shipwreck and was devoured by the darkness. Her heart pounded as her mind wrestled with fears of what she might find.

♦

The torch crackled in Liz's hand. She walked through the corridors of the lower decks. The walls were covered in rust, chipped white paint, and pipes hung with bulbous fungi and algae that gave off a humid, stomach-churning scent.

Pale crabs scurried away from the light. They were larger than they should be, mutated by the magic, with overgrown claws and tumors pulsing from between the gaps in their exoskeletons. The stranger grimaced at the horrific evidence of what magic could do.

It was not a big ship—a research vessel couldn't be— but it felt like a labyrinth. She came to a crooked ladder halfway down the corridor. Water dripped periodically from up. She raised the torch and peered up into the darkness, but couldn't see anything of the upper deck. She looked back down the corridor. It dipped down into a pool of black water.

With a pounding in her chest, she gripped the ladder and ascended up.

◆

A metal door groaned before creaking open. The torchlight sent scattered shadows across the chamber. She'd found the ship's galley. A few tables were thrown against one side, plates and forks caught in a pile of growing fungus and more mutated crabs.

Liz crossed the uneven floor, her entire world caught in a Dutch angle. A row of lockers was bolted to the other side of the room. Roaches as big as human hands fled from the torchlight.

Liz found nothing in the first locker. In the second, only mold. *This place is a fucking rotting tomb.* She opened the third locker and paused.

A picture still clung to a magnet. It was a photo of the crew of the RRS *Magellan*. It was a photo of the crew of the RRS Magellan. Seven people stood in front of the ship, wearing T-shirts, jeans, and smiles. They stood in front of the ship. T-shirts, jeans, khakis, and smiles. A camera meant modernity, power, and wealth. Wealth that Dunwich hoarded while the rest of the country languished in a feudal backwardness. Nobles like Lord Nors kept it that way.

I can't help that now.

She brought the photo closer to her face. In the hands of the oldest researcher was an glimmering of a crystal orb, half wrapped in fabric and held like a cherished item. Whatever they had done on their voyage, they'd brought something back.

Something clanged; she looked up. A shadow moved in the kitchen mess. She ground her teeth. She knew he was there; she could feel *his* eyes on her. Her ghost. She saw him standing in a doorway, partially hidden, his sword dripping blood.

"Get the fuck out of here!" she hissed, fighting the urge to run.

He stared back, unmoving beneath his cowl.

Liz, without looking away from the ghost, put the photo in her pocket. Hands trembling, she gripped her revolver, raised it, aimed, and fired. The ghost vanished within the blinding flash.

"Fucking asshole." She knew who he was. She had killed him. He was the first person she ever killed. She holstered the weapon, closing and unclosing her fist to keep from trembling.

Liz forced herself further into the shipwreck. I *have to face this. I have to face this.* It became her prayer. *I have to face this.* The magic grew stronger.

◆

She climbed a ladder that led into the wheelhouse of the ship. All the windows were blown out, and the fresh, salty air whistled in. She inhaled and the haze of magic on her tongue abated slightly. She looked up through one of the shattered windows. Castle Nors loomed overhead, a bastion of decay.

Glass crunched under Liz's boots. She circled the helm of the ship, eyeing the computer console that housed the radio, radar, and other devices. All of the electronics were broken.

She glanced back toward the entrance, eyes watching warily for the cloaked man. Was he real? He couldn't be. *He's dead.* Could it be the magic of the ship? Could it bring her thoughts to life? Could it even make her thoughts physical?

The one major failing of her training: she was completely illiterate when it came to magic. The stranger didn't understand it. She had never been around wizards or warlocks or anyone with a genuine connection to the unnatural forces. Her Master was a monk. He had dealt with the spiritual and,when it suited him, the practical disciplines of martial arts and fighting ability. Magic was alien. Magic was still as distant to her as it had been the day the cloaked men Exposed her to the Wrong Side.

"You'll face things you won't believe or understand," her Master had told her.

Now she understood what he meant. She rubbed her temple, feeling a headache growing.

She circled back to the rear walls of the room.

There was a desk covered in graphs. Along the wall were plastic panels and cork boards. She looked up, seeing the routes and information vital to the ship. Paper crunched beneath her boot. She kneeled down and scanned the discarded documents. Many were unreadable, either rotted or scratched out.

...Illegal act of...broken indigenous sovereignty... cursed the expedition.

...Dunwich supports our actions...

...imperialist...

...Pre-Colombian artifact secured...homebound...

...mistake.

Liz lifted a smeared piece of paper. A piece of a dossier with printed photos of a glassy skull at various angles. There were notes in the margins. *MR-3 battery. No evidence of carving. Grown?* Then at the bottom, in ugly panicked letters: *Nightmares made manifest.*

She looked back up. Amongst the faded documents pinned to the cork boards was a diagram, curled and stained, of the ship. The diagram was marked with a circle at the furthest corner of the hull, a location deep within the engine block.

Liz sighed. She knew exactly where that was. It was down the corridor she had passed and through one of the flooded sections of the ship.

She hurried down ladders and through the corridors and abandoned decks, spiraling back deeper into the tomb of the RRS *Magellan.*

She swung around a bend; there was an open hatch just in front of her, a ladder on her left.

She froze.

The pulsing in Liz's head grew more intense.

A blood-slicked blade had appeared in the torchlight.

Heavy combat boots stepped onto the metal grating. A huge figure enveloped in a black cloak came into view, his cowl concealing his face.

Liz held the torch out defensively, her other hand falling to her firearm. "You're not real. You're not real."

He took a powerful step forward. The metal grating shuddered. The vibrations crawled up her leg. *No. No. No.* But she did feel it. *He's not real. He's not real. He's not real.*

The second foot landed. The metal platform shuddered again.

She fired the revolver. The flash illuminated the ragged cut of his cloak and his square, stubbled jaw. He didn't vanish. He didn't move. He didn't die.

She fired again.

Nothing.

Another.

He's not real!

She dropped the torch and it fell into the corridor below; the light dimmed and the shadows grew. The cloaked warrior became a giant. The shadows enwrapped and empowered him. The stranger felt very small.

She held the gun in both hands.

She screamed, "Just fucking die!" She unloaded the revolver until the hammer clicked empty. Desperation took over her, running in full force.

The tall man raised his stained blade—The sword of chalky black metal. The wolves set into the hilt seemed bigger and more vicious than ever, snarling and snapping like the creatures of nightmares. Monstrous hounds as hungry as the murderous men in their black cloaks. He brought the blade down.

Liz dove away from the strike, grabbing the ladder. The blade struck the grating, slicing into the platform. The metal of the ladder was so rusted and warped that it broke under the jolt. Liz lost her grip and fell into the corridor below. She landed hard in the sand. Mutated crabs scuttled away.

She wheezed, her lungs clapping shut in her chest. She coughed, spat on the sand, and rolled back onto her feet. When she looked up, the swordsman was gone. Her torch was dying in the sand. The knitted shadows spread across Liz's face.

She finally let out a gasp.

"I killed you; you're dead." She gripped the hilt of her sword. "I took your sword. Your cloak. Your life."

Her voice echoed down the metallic hull of the ship.

And a voice answered.

"And what does that have to do with anything?"

Her breath caught in her throat. *It's just the magic. Just this vile place.* She turned down the corridor. It slanted downward into sitting sea water. Crabs scuttled around the putrid layers of algae.

She stood at the edge of the water. "I'll show you exactly what it means."

Liz dropped her cloak and belt, creating a bundle of them and her revolver which she set on a jagged pipe hanging from the wall. Kneeling, Liz took out one of the condoms she had purchased from the peddler. She tore it open and blew it into a pocket. She threw terrified glances over her shoulder as she worked. She put her bandages, tinder, and box of matches into the rubber pouch before tying it shut and stuffing it into her pocket.

When she was ready, she drew her sword from its scabbard. The long blade of chalky black metal refused to glint in the low light of the tunnel.

She took the sword in a reverse grip before wadding into the water. The icy water crept up her waist and groin, then up her shirt, sending chills through her. "Fuck all of you," she hissed, before gasping in a final breath and diving into the black water.

◆

As she swam through the flooded corridor, in the total darkness, strands of kelp tickled her arms and stomach. Terrified chills went up her spine and she swam harder. Through the watery crypt she felt a man's gloved hand grab at her ankle. She tore through it with her sword. Fear drove her forward. She felt more desperate than she had in any fight before.

Liz burst from the water and into the next corridor, gasping for air. She gagged, choked, and vomited onto the deck. The sour was everywhere. The wrongness of everything. She reached around for something to anchor herself, but found only more sand-covered floor. She found the bulkhead wall and dragged herself onto the floor. She spat out water and wiped the grime from her face. Her braid had come undone, leaving her with tangles of black hair clinging to her cheeks.

She spat again, gasped for air, before retching again. She inhaled and exhaled, forcing the humid, putrid air to fill her lungs.

The blackness of the chamber stretched around her. A womb of complete darkness with rippling energies around her, the stink of magic, the rot of atomic forces. Her stomach churned as she felt the tendrils of alien power touching her.

I still have you. She squeezed the grip of her sword, solid and cold, to anchor herself.

She coughed again, finding her strength outside the fear. *It'll pass.* She shook herself of water before reaching into her pocket for the condom. She flicked her hand dry before ripping open the rubber.

A clatter of metal echoed through the darkness.

A terrified, "Fuck, fuck, fuck!" slipped from her lips. She fumbled, dropping a match onto the wet sand. She heard getting closer. A man's chuckle broke through the darkness. She pulled another match and managed to get it to light. It burst into a frail tongue of light.

The chamber was completely silent.

The engine room rose up around Liz like a cathedral. It had upper balconies that overlooked the generators. The carcasses of two dilapidated engine blocks sat against the far wall, leaning in like broken columns of a mausoleum, covered in nests of warped metal. Mutated bulbs of algae hung from the ceiling like fetid stalactites; mutated crabs, bulbous and corrupted, waddled through the gloom.

Liz stood up, sword at her side, the tiny light in her hand. It was seconds from burning out.

The contents of a maintenance rack lay scattered along the side of the chamber. She cupped the burning match and rushed to the shelf. She found a broken flashlight. *Useless.* With the match burnt almost to her fingertips, she found an oil canister. She tore off the remains of her sleeve, wrapped it around the end of a broken broom handle, and poured the thick sludge over the drenched fabric.

The match bit her fingers, forcing her to drop it. It died the instant it touched the floor, shutting her into darkness once again.

In her mad scramble to get another match, she heard movement. It was the encroaching attack from her worst nightmares. *Thunk. Thunk. Thunk. Thunk.* The heavy footfalls of a predator stalking its prey.

Her mind was thrown back to her worst day. *The* worst day. One bad thing after another. It was the day she had been cast into a world beyond her comprehension, a world where monsters and magic really existed. Her own world cast aside as folklore and mythology flooded in. Worse still, a world where society itself was cast back into the violence and pain of the middle ages.

She saw the bus burning in the night, tendrils of flames reaching to the night sky. Later she would learn about Mass Exposures— isolated groups of people, even entire towns, cast into the Wrong Side by bands of murders or monster tribes for their own purposes.

Liz remembered being with someone. Maybe two

people. People she cared about. People she loved. People she had hurt. She just couldn't remember them. The men with the black cloaks and black swords, they did this. They had brought her here. Not for any reason or purpose other than their enjoyment of her pain.

She finally got the match to light. The torch exploded into light, so bright it caused her to wince.

The footsteps stopped.

When she looked up, she saw a dead face, pale and pockmarked, rushing away from the light.

Liz jumped back, holding back a scream. *Fuck you.* She held the torch high, casting the light across the broken husk of the engine room. She peered into the gap between the dead engines. The rotten smell, the magic, continued to grow stronger. It drew her in. She grit her teeth.

"You're just another monster," said the stranger. "Worse than an animal. You all delighted in your ability to murder people like sheep. You reveled in it." She glared at the darkened space between the engine blocks. The glow of her torch revealed a pathway between warped and twisted metal.

"You know nothing, girl," rasped the voice.

"I've learned a lot in five years," she replied. "I know that in a desperate world, people become monsters."

"You've learned nothing."

"I've learned plenty. I've learned how dark this world can be and how to survive it. I've learned that I took what I lost for granted. I should have protected it, appreciated it...but I didn't know it would be taken away from me like that."

She walked toward the pathway between the broken metal monoliths. Beyond was a half-open doorway into a storage room. Liz could feel the energy emanating from within the portal.

The man in the black cloak appeared in the pathway between the engine blocks. The hulking shoulders, a face of shadow, boots and fists of iron. He clutched the wolf-hilted sword casually, blood still dripping from the chalky black blade.

His chuckle echoed through the shadows. *"The dogs will bite, the wolves will stalk, and jackals will feast on your corpse, girl."*

Fear crawled up her spine and she screamed. She felt a feral need to escape. Liz had walked into one of her nightmares. *That's what this magic does, isn't it?* It brought nightmares to life, reflecting one's inner darkness across reality like light through a prism. She gripped her sword and torch with white knuckled desperation. She wouldn't run. *Not this time.*

"You'll die girl. Alone. Just like you lived. Alone. Forgotten. Then dead like the rest. Dead like your family."

"I won't let you haunt me anymore," she hissed. "I won't let you keep me up at night. I won't let you and your friends keep doing what you've done." She dropped the torch and fell into a low guard. "I killed you and now I am trapped in this world."

He stood motionless.

"I will find you. All of you."

"And what will you do then?" rasped the voice. *"Will you run like you did?"*

She gasped, taking a step back as the memory rushed back into her.

"Like when you left your family to be slaughtered?"

She hissed, forcing another step forward. "I will find all of you and put you down like the dogs you are." *For myself and for everyone else you've hurt.* She glared at the room where the artifact was housed. She needed to reach it. "You're in my way."

She burst into motion, springing off her toes. Sword in both hands, she flew through the air, screaming. He raised his sword in defense.

Metal clanged.

Liz's eyes widened. She had expected the apparition to dissolve or reveal itself to be nothing but a vision. *The nightmare made manifest,* she thought as their blades locked. He pushed against her guard with all the dominating force she'd dreaded he would have.

"I'm not the woman you met all those years ago!" She danced around his guard and impaled him on her sword, puncturing his armour and scraping his ribs with the blade. He rasped and fell to the ground, limp and bloody like the day he died.

She exhaled, releasing everything; all her fear, terror, and exhaustion.

"Did you think it would be so easy?" echoed the voice.

She looked up and her mouth opened with horror.

Another cloaked swordsman. This one had spikes on his armor and a breastplate faced with Kevlar. *"There were more of us that night. You only managed to get the drop on one of us."*

The warrior dropped onto the path in front of the door. *"You don't know who we are."*

She charged, screaming with frustrated fury. Weapons clanged. The apparition fell as Liz's sword slashed through his shoulder and into his chest. The body collapsed.

Another appeared. Tall, burly, and bearded. *"You have no idea."*

A third stood on the engine block above, thin, holding two small swords. Another, fur around his collar, waiting along the pathway with a black longsword. *"We are the reapers. We are the hunters, and we will be your death."*

Liz ran for the storage room. Just before she reached it, an arm reached out from the darkness of the chamber. The first swordsmen, the one she had killed, the one who haunted her nightmares, stepped out. He was taller than before; his shoulders filled the portal. Behind him, a deep, unworldly glow rippled from the darkness. The artifact screamed its projections, fighting for its surreal reality.

The warriors surrounded her, dropping from above and appearing from behind the engine block. They would just keep coming until they got her. She couldn't fight forever. She would be overwhelmed eventually.

In her nightmares, they came for her like a horde of demons and eventually overwhelmed her, defeating her no matter how hard she fought. This time, she wouldn't wake up when they killed her...

She held her guard as the swordsmen surrounded her. In their cloaks they looked like wraiths. With a desperate attack, she swung at the swordsman in her way.

Their blades connected. He countered by punching her in the face.

Liz flew backwards, her face bloodied and cracked. She rose; driving her sword into the floor, she forced herself to her feet. Tears filled her eyes and Liz glared at the apparitions. *I won't let him win.*

They held their swords upwards, surrounding her like a garden of blades.

Liz raised her sword in a high guard, arms straining to hold the heavy blade. *When did it get so heavy?* How long could she keep fighting with a weapon growing heavy and useless?

They moved to impale her with a dozen swords. *I can't fight all of them...* She was so exhausted. So tired of the nightmares. She just wanted to rest...the nightmare of living on the Wrong Side could be over.

Past the first swordsman, the open door of the storage room revealed the hiding spot of the artifact.

On a crate sat a lead-lined box. The otherworldly light gleamed from within.

Liz, through the tears, saw the prize. A small human skull, made of a perfectly clear crystal. A pre-Columbian artifact of holy significance to a distant culture. The crew of the Magellan had stolen it, breaking treaties and foreign sovereignty.

The swordsmen moved to rip her to pieces. All the horrible acts she dreaded they would do if she failed, all the things her nightmares promised they would do. To tear her limbs from her body, shave her scalp, cut off her lips and break her neck.

She screamed and lobbed the sword with both hands.

It whistled through the air, spinning end over end. The swordsman swerved away from it, but she hadn't been aiming for him. She could never defeat her nightmares. They always won in the end.

He turned at the last second. The ghosts' blades were inches from Liz's neck.

The sword slammed into the lead box. The crystal skull cracked in half.

The colourless light cut out as though a switch had been flipped. The swords vanished. The figures cut out like a changed channel. A rush of air ripped through the dusty tomb.

Liz was alone. The haze, the taste, the magic, was gone. The only sounds were the crackle of the torch and the splash of the ocean against the ship's hull.

Liz exhaled, falling to her hands and knees. Tears streamed down her face; she gasped, the fear lifting from her back. The nightmare was over.

Once recovered, she wiped the blood and grime from her face and entered the storage room.

Her sword had cracked the skull like an egg. Whatever the blade was made of, it was stronger than the artifact. Shards lay scattered over the crate.

She picked up her sword, nodding to the wolves on the hilt as though they had saved her.

Midway through turning to leave, she stopped. She frowned, seeing skeletons scattered across the chamber. Piled among the crates and supplies were the bodies of the curse's victim—scorched, blackened skeletons. Consumed by the artifact and its curse, their flesh had been vaporized.

She couldn't save the lost townsfolk, but she had stopped the curse from destroying any more lives.

She marched out of the shipwreck.

♦

Fatigue dragged at Liz's legs and eyes. She exited the shipwreck, mechanically moving one foot in front of the other. She was exhausted, numb, and starving. Sunrise broke through the retreating clouds. It was the dawn of a new day.

She walked back toward the inn, cloak thrown over her

shoulder, scabbard and holster hung at her sides. She looked like hell. A shout echoed from a window; someone had seen her exiting the shipwreck. The awakening townsfolk paused with shocked gasps, muttering gossip, and horrible suspicion, as she passed by. They didn't expect anyone to walk out of that tomb.

Without realizing it, Liz had entered the inn. The smell of food drifted into the common room from the kitchen.

The stranger took a spot at the bar, setting her soaked cloak and weapons on the stool beside her. Marsha appeared; eyes wide, shocked to see the stranger in her current state.

"Breakfast," said the stranger.

Marsha stood frozen, eyes glistening. There was a long pause as Marsha put the pieces together. At last she asked, in a cracking voice, "My son?"

The stranger shook her head.

Marsha gasped before letting out a long breath. The hope she had been holding out for her son deflated with her lungs. The truth was the curse ate the ones it stole.

The stranger rested her head on the bar top. She closed her eyes, feeling lighter than she had in all the years since her Exposure.

LIES IN NEON

Sometimes you have to do something bad. Sometimes you have to do something distasteful to survive in this world.

Sometimes you have to be the bad guy in someone else's story.

That's what Kcaz always told himself. Another day, another beating, another dollar. He hammered his fist into the fragile human princeling. Lord Barnard crumpled against the oak desk. The office was a cramped windowless cell, the walls lined with ledger shelves and a huge hand-painted portrait of a Franco Aristocrat on the back wall.

"Where the fuck is Blue Orchid?" Kcaz held Lord Barnard against the desk.

"I don't know what you're talking about, you fucking crazy orc. I don't know."

Kcaz lifted the human, fragile as a doll. "You're going to tell me where Blue Orchid is," Kcaz bared his fangs in the human's face, "and who they really are."

"I don't know."

Kcaz's patience was growing exceptionally thin today. He was a broad-shouldered orc with a thin face, a claw mark over his jaw, and a bite taken out of his left ear. His dark green skin was scratched up like old leather. Kcaz wore a charcoal suit with a black tie. A true wolf in sheep's clothing.

"I don't have enough time for Franco Expats playing politics."

Lord Barnard was a princeling from some minor house in Franco. Plenty of second sons, daughters, cousins, and bastards of noble families came from the eastern kingdoms to the Underground for business ventures, education, and to spread their tendrils in the local scene. *Fucking Expats, all of them.*

Kcaz wrenched the human's arm outward, thin as a twig. He placed Barnard's finger in a cigar slicer. "I'm going to ask again. Where is Blue Orchid?"

"I don't know!" repeated Barnard, unable to move. He struggled in Kcaz's irresistible grip. "I'll pay you. I'll pay you anything you want. Just let me go. I don't know who you're talking about."

"Then why is he paying you thirty thousand credits monthly?" Kcaz brought his fist down on the slicer.

With the wet thunk of a chopped carrot, the finger jumped onto the floor. Barnard screamed, clutching his bleeding hand. He jabbered incoherent threats at the orc. Kcaz dropped a handkerchief at Barnard's feet. "Put pressure on that. I expect you in my office with the information I'm looking for by the end of the week." Kcaz collected his hat off the hook on the wall and left Barnard's office.

A terrified secretary cowered behind a desk in the other room. Kcaz nodded to the young woman. "Good day, miss. I'd advise calling the nearest Medica—Lord Barnard has had an accident."

He left the office, still stuck on the case. He went through the doors of the office spire. The security guards, two of them orcs themselves, glared at Kcaz. He stepped out of the spire. A beetle shell-like vehicle on glowing blue repulsors flew overhead. The neon and chrome of the city enveloped Kcaz like he was an insect.

The Underground. Nyrvellir. Clan Country. Realm of the Goblin King. The biggest metropolis on Earth, lying within the Rokki Mountains. The peaks of corporate spires filled the hollow mountain cavern. Kcaz walked along an avenue. In the distance, across the field of spires, apartment complexes, and mall courtyards, rose an immense PillarTower—a megastructure that held the mountain together with buttresses of steel and roots of concrete. Businesses, shanties, and expansions climbed the trunk like a hyper capitalist fungal growth.

Kcaz reached the metro station and put in his earbuds to drown out the deafening noise. The din of trains, cellphones, crying children, shouting voices, and a million other sounds were too much for his overly sensitive ears. He slipped into the first subway home and played a Phillip K. Dick audiobook as the subway jerked into motion.

He closed his hazel eyes and let the rumble of the subway rock him into a half-sleeping daze as he headed home. Back to the Eighth District.

♦

The door swung open to Kcaz's office-apartment, revealing bare plaster walls, a table with a radio and coffeemaker, and his desk piled with case files. Against the back wall were two towering cabinets flanking the only hint of colour in the room: a small shelf of paperback novels.

He flipped on the radio.

A cackling voice came through the speakers, "…and this one goes out to all those boys out there just clawing and biting their way to the top. Here is some Julie London. *Cry Me a River.* This is Armistice 97.2."

Kcaz fell into his chair, exhausted. He hadn't slept in almost forty-eight hours. He needed sleep. He picked up the Blue Orchid file, stared at it, then cast it aside and opened the bottom drawer of his desk with the apprehension of a recruit with a hand grenade. A bottle of Caledonian whiskey stared back at him.

The sad song continued to play on the radio. The slow bass of it crept into Kcaz's heart. He'd have sung along if he had the cords for it. *Dumb orcs don't sing.* He closed the drawer and glanced at the calendar. *Day two-hundred and sixty-one. Another day. Always just another day.*

A knock rapped against his door. Through the frosted glass of the window, he saw the silhouette of a human woman.

Here we go again, thought Kcaz. Sleep would have to wait.

Kcaz checked the top drawer for his firearm, a RC 1919 .50 caliber. A weapon designed specifically for orcs. It had enough stopping power to stagger a charging rhino.

"What is it?"

The woman's voice cooed, "Is this the detective?"

"The door's unlocked."

With a click and a whoosh, the woman entered the office-apartment. She wore a long black dress with a slit

154

down the side. Her dark lips in a slight frown, hair swirled and set with an offset black hat and veil. Her deep cleavage was framed with a sparkling necklace. She could have been a golden age movie star on the Right Side.

"What can I do for you, miss?"

"I need help, sir."

"Please, sit."

She sat on the edge of his desk. Her rose perfume strangled Kcaz's senses.

Here we go.

"May I smoke?" She held up a golden-tipped roll.

"No," said Kcaz, completely unamused. "What's your name?"

"Samantha Mae McCarthy," she swooned. "My husband," she threw her head back in sorrow, "He…he…" She was playing up the heartbreak.

Kcaz didn't take his eyes off of her. *This ought to be good.* Was the husband cheating? Had he run away with the mistress? Taken the children? Kcaz managed to detect the pheromones through the synthetic floral stench; he knew exactly what kind of bullshit he was about to be fed.

She pulled a slip of paper from her cleavage and shoved it in Kcaz's face.

155

"You've been served."

I've been wrong before. He took the document; his eyes scanned the official suit. It was from the Central District's attorney office. *Fucking UpTown scum.* He had done work for a noble family in the Third District and had uncovered more dirty laundry than expected—the family had not taken kindly to that. Now they were suing his green ass for defamation.

"Fuck."

"Apparently not," said Samantha Mae McCarthy.

Kcaz looked at her flatly. "You know, trying to seduce an orc is like sitting on a cucumber—you just look desperate."

"It worked though, didn't it?" she laughed, "You were leaning on every word."

"Get out."

She slunk out of the office, not even half as elegantly as she had entered.

Kcaz slammed his fist against the desk, the document gripped in his claws. The entire room shook, and the radio hiccupped. Some of the other files on Kcaz's desk fell to the floor.

"Fuck this suit."

Slam.

"Fuck this office."

Slam.

"And fuck you Samantha Mae McCarthy," he roared. He opened the bottom drawer, looked at the whiskey, and slammed it shut. Another day. *Just one more day.*

A wordless roar escaped his mouth.

He reached under the desk for the hatchet he kept hidden for emergencies and lobbed it at the far wall. It stuck into the plaster.

"Fuck!"

He had lost his temper and now he had a wall to fix. *Better the wall than an administrative adept...*

The phone rang.

He picked up the receiver. "What?!"

"Hey, Kcaz," said a familiar voice, "It's Officer Cadus from the Eleventh District Police Department. We're wondering if you have time to come downtown. There's Clan work that requires your attention."

Ah shit. Sleep would have to wait.

◆

The street closed in like a mineshaft with a low ceiling; apartment stoops and shops leaned in or dug under the street. The walls were splattered with graffiti, the gutters flooded with trash. Kcaz eyed the likely trajectories of the blasts that had come from the upper floor apartments. The husks of three trucks sat on the downtown avenue like kills on the savannah.

The street reeked of vaporized ozone—burnt iron and chemicals. Whatever the thieves had used, it was far more advanced than anything a handful of thugs ought to have had access to. It was also impossible to track manufacturers in a place as big and complex as the Underground.

Kcaz kicked a piece of charred debris, his mind already working out that he needed to look for the seller first, not the manufacturer.

Officer Cadus handed Kcaz a cup of coffee.

"Thanks."

Cadus was a Carib-born human, raised in the Underground from infancy. *Must have broken his mother's heart when he became a cop*, thought Kcaz. The orc assumed Cadus was handsome for a human. He had a strong jaw and short curly hair. He wore a long coat over his suit. His fedora ducked downward slightly.

"Why am I here, Cadus? You said it was Clan work? Looks like just another hit for some loot."

Cadus walked up to an apartment building—exactly where Kcaz guessed the thieves had set up their weapons. Kcaz followed the officer in.

Inside the building was a graffiti-marred lobby. In the sitting area were three goblins, two sat elegantly and the third lay on the floor, clutching at what Kcaz assumed to be broken ribs. The tiny rat-like creature was also bleeding from a gash over his eyes.

The seated goblins rose to greet Officer Cadus and Kcaz. They wore pinstripe suits tailored to their size, pointed shoes, and peaked fedoras. One had a long nose and drooping ears, the other was bloated as a tumor and sported a pinched nose. They both wore the emblems of the DarkHart Clan on their lapels.

Cadus took his leave, bowing as he did so. Kcaz was left alone with the pair of bosses, their latest victim still sprawled out on the floor.

The huge orc gulped.

"I'll get to the point," said the tumorous one. "Kcaz Skry, we just got hit by a band of too-hungry boys. They stole three million in platinum that was coming from our refinery and going to the Otomo Syndicate for pay."

"Yes, boss."

The goblin waddled up to Kcaz, face jiggling as he did.

He barely reached the huge orc's waist. "The cops can find the thugs easily enough, but it's the mastermind behind this that we need found."

"Yes, boss."

"This imp—" he glanced at the landlord dying on the floor, "—took cash and didn't ask for names from our band of cretins. What's your clan, runt?"

The bleeding goblin coughed. "The GreenStrikes, boss. I—"

"Well, your boss is getting a talk from me tonight."

Kcaz looked down at the poor creature. His lax attitude towards his tenets would bring the DarkHart's wrath upon his clan-brothers. Not that he would be alive to see it.

The lead goblin turned back to Kcaz. "Find the weapons, and find the goddamn fucking imp who planned this. That's all you're good for, Skry."

"Yes, boss."

"Now get out of our sight."

Kcaz nodded. As he left the lobby, he threw a curious glance over his shoulder. Above, one of the tenants, a little Latin girl, watched as the droopy-eared goblin drew a garrotte wire from his coat. The bleeding imp whimpered for mercy. Her mother pulled her back into the upstairs apartment.

Kcaz closed the door.

Cadus was waiting outside for him, smoking a cigarette. He looked at Kcaz. "And?"

"You're going to find the imps that did this," said Kcaz. "I'm going to track down whoever planned it."

Cadus's eyes narrowed. He looked confused.

"You've been on the beat, what, three years?" asked Kcaz.

Cadus nodded.

"Small time stuff mostly?"

Cadus nodded again.

"Who's the Chief Inspector of the Eleventh District?"

"Boss Garas...of the DarkHart Clan."

"Well," said Kcaz, "let me fill you in, given that your bosses didn't. When something big like this happens, they need someone independent to track down the culprit." Kcaz pulled out his phone and started checking his emails; the Blue Orchid case would have to wait. "What happens when it turns out to be some CorpLord or a rival Clan?

They can't exactly have Clan-controlled police going after them. They have to maintain the balance between forces."

He looked at Cadus. The human's build could have been that of a soldier, but down here he had to settle for being an officer of the Goblin King's law. "So they send a sucker like me to root around until a real case can be made and taken to the HighClans."

Cadus sneered. "Fine. I'll keep you in the loop. Hope you do the same."

Fat chance. "It will take time to sell the platinum piece by piece through various buyers and intermediaries—weeks, or even months. That is our only saving grace."

"We'll keep an eye out for it."

"Whatever."

Kcaz headed to the one place he knew he could track down an orc flush with cash: the Eighth District. Finding a particular orc there, however, was like finding a needle in a dozen haystacks.

♦

The Underground was an organism—the meanest, ugliest, and nastiest fungal spread the gods ever decided to curse the earth with. In the tenth century, with the early forays of Eurofolk to the Americas, bands of dwarves had managed to begin their process of colonising the Rokki

Mountains. They'd kept to themselves and ignored the pleas of Indigenous peoples when the Latins arrived. Karma came for the Dwergs eventually.

By the twentieth century, the colony had grown to stretch from the foothills of Alaska to the mountainous badlands to the south. It was called Nyrvellir, a modern semi-democratic realm within the mountains. That was, until the influenza pandemic of nineteen-eighteen mutated during its passage through The Veil. It had decimated the dwarves unlike anything they'd seen before, a culling so great that the Nyrvellir government collapsed.

The mountains ate their builders. The Rokkis had a life of their own, untamed from their unfathomable depths to their unreachable peaks. They betrayed everyone.

Factions had flooded the emptied mountain holds. Goblins, orcs, vampires...immigrants of every denomination were affected. The 1920s, by Gregorian, were dominated by the various wars and power struggles between those powers. Dozens of kings and coalitions devoured by the mountains until the Goblin Clans came out on top.

Now, nearly a hundred and fifty million people lived in the hollowed out Rocky Mountains of North America. Most of them got eaten by the mountains sooner or later.

Just don't get eaten, thought Kcaz. That's all anyone could hope for in the Underground. It felt like sullen resignation as he stepped into the biggest mess hall in the Eighth District, 3rd Ward. He checked his watch. *Over fifty hours without sleep.* That's the thing about the Underground—no day or night cycle. One can lose themselves in the perpetual grime and darkness.

The mess hall was as big as four football pitches, with long rows of cement tables and benches filled with hundreds of green, grey, and chestnut-brown orcs. Hordes made up of small clans, bands from larger tribes, or isolated outcasts. There were long walls filled with hundreds of different shops and kitchens. The smells of grease, spices, bubbling fat, and crackling meats drifted to Kcaz's senses. He hadn't eaten in a while.

"Mmmm," hummed Kcaz, "smells like home."

This was the best place to start on the hunt for a boy flush with platinum.

Kcaz went to his favourite noodle joint first. The shop's glass panel was covered in steam from boiling pasta baskets, the flat top covered in burnt vegetable ends. He stood with his hands in his pockets. He could feel eyes on his back. He turned to look.

Three runts from the Redjay Clan glared at Kcaz. He rose to his full height of nearly seven feet, lips pulled pack in an intimidating snarl. They moved on.

He reached the front of the line.

"Kcaz! My friend!" squeaked the woman at the till, a tiny Viet woman named Mai. "Pork noodles?"

"You're the best." He leaned in. "Got a question for you."

A grin spread across her face. She always gave Kcaz the gossip he needed—for a few credits.

"Any boys mention platinum or anti-armour weaponry?"

"Try Pott's," said Mai with a snicker.

Kcaz added a few extra credits to her tip.

"Always so kind."

Kcaz took his tray of noodles. The strips of *real pork*, not synthetic, sizzled with the smell of soy, garlic, and ginger. Whoever was backing Mai's little shop had certainly given her quite the budget to work with. Kcaz passed the long tables filled with orcs.

A small-time chieftain declared his supremacy over a table. He ordered some runts too scared to disagree with him to get more chili oil.

Dogs, cats, rats, and other stray animals were not uncommon sights below the tables. A thug cooed at one of the mutts as he scratched it behind the ears. An ancient shaman with fingers like knobs of wood begged for change.

Kcaz eventually found a spot. When he sat down, a clutch of BlueTongue orcs got up and left. He sat quietly eating his noodles. Around him, the constant chaos of fights, threats, and hushed whispers churned like the primal stew that the Eighth District was. Orcs were not segregated in the strictest sense, would never be officially confined to their zone, but it was a struggle for them outside their ghetto. *Good luck to the lad applying for an apartment anywhere without a patron.* Kcaz caught a handful of runts from The Dag glaring at him. He offered them another threatening snarl.

Kcaz was without a Clan. He had been an outcast since the day he was born, found by human mercenaries in the foothills of the Rokki Mountains.

His ears twitched at a change in movement around him.

Kcaz whipped around and caught the wrist of one of the runts. A shiv was clutched in the tiny hand. Kcaz was nearly three times the size of the boy. The donkey-faced orc squealed, trying to pull himself free, but Kcaz towered over the runt like a darkened mountain. He threw his forehead forward, head-butting the runt and knocking him to the ground.

Kcaz roared like a lion disarming a rival, spit and

debris flying off his fangs. The batch of runts ran, tripping over one another as they did.

Just another day in the Eighth.

He left his half-eaten noodles to be scavenged by the outcasts. He swam through the rows of tables toward Pott's. A meat pie shop.

The human baker who had seen the exchange of violence cowered as Kcaz approached. "Not me, boss, I got nothing for you."

Kcaz leaned over the tiny flour-splattered man. "You heard anything about platinum? Anything about some weapons?"

"Not one bit, sir," said the human.

"Nothing?"

"Yes, boss."

"No orcs mention a job in the Eleventh?"

"No, Boss. I—I only know about a swimmer, uptown from here. Mentioned a big job in the Eleventh. He took a pie. Gave a tip. Skinny fella', pale as milk, sir."

"Fine," said Kcaz. "Thank you."

Kcaz stalked away, feeling the rush of the hunt trying to worm its way into him.

♦

The lift doors slid open and Kcaz stepped into the den. He shuddered and looked down: he had stepped in a puddle of vomit. *Fuck! These were real leather.* Around him flowed a jungle of cables and wires; computer terminals the size of boulders were scattered throughout the debris of empty takeout containers and garbage.

Swimmers were scattered amongst the terminals in their nests and enclaves, screens and keyboards littered amongst the chaos. The blue haze of pheromones and body odor filled the air. Kcaz felt his stomach churn as he stalked through the forest. He could see some swimmers leaning into their screens with bloodshot eyes, others were wearing insectoid headsets for a virtual reality uplink.

Kcaz found one girl without a VR headset. She wore a bikini top and shorts and sat at a desk. Her ergonomic chair looked like a throne. She sipped on an energy drink as she howled over a radio set.

Kcaz sat on an empty stool.

"The fuck you talking about?" she screamed, half-unaware of Kcaz's presence. "The stock was over forty! Now *one fucking guy dies* and you want to pull out? No wonder your wife can't get pregnant!"

Her bloodshot eyes nearly jumped out of her skull when she saw Kcaz.

When the internet had come to the Wrong Side, it had to be copied, recreated, and rebuilt for a new plane of existence. Once the uplink between Clan tech-firms, Nipponi syndicates, and a few stations in Europa were established, the developed parts of the world were thrust into the twenty-first century. Mass media was changing the Wrong Side unlike anything had before.

"I'll call you back," she hissed. She threw down the headset. "How can I help you, boss?"

Kcaz put his identification on the desk. She threw aside empty pop cans as she took it, studying it closely.

"I'm searching for someone involved with a raid in the Eleventh. Someone handling anti-armour weapons."

Her eyes glinted. "I can certainly ask around. Heard the DarkHarts are quite embarrassed. They're trying to hold off the feeds from carrying the story," she smiled and handed the ID back. "Clans are always so paranoid about perceived weakness, eh?"

"Yes. No one around here handles that kind of thing?"

She glanced further through the jungle of the den. "Ask Guy. Guy au Europa. Trash twit likes to play in fields he shouldn't."

"Which one is he?"

"You'll see."

Kcaz nodded. "Thank you, miss." He sniffed. "You may want to take a shower."

"Fuck off, greenie."

Kcaz chuckled and prowled through the den. It was located in a stalactite above the Eighth District's MidTown, like an upside-down skyscraper. The den was located in the point of the spire; its windows peered over the city below. The Eighth District lacked the neon and colour of other districts in the Underground. It boomed with the clash of industrial work, the cry of fighting pits, and the roar of the arenas.

Kcaz could see his neighbourhood from here. His entire ward was little more than a pockmark in the underground dystopia.

He found Guy au Europa entombed in a full-bodied VR cockpit, naked except for a pair of shorts. Lying back in an ergonomic coffin, his fingers were set with electric nodes, his head encased in a beetle shell headset. He had a Saxony flag splattered on the side of his cockpit. Guy looked like a skeleton playing at being a man, his sunken ribs and pelvis clearly visible.

Kcaz knocked on the helmet.

"Fuck. What the fuck!" the mask opened up,

revealing the sunken skull of a man with wild bloodshot eyes.

"I got questions for you," said Kcaz, holding up his identification.

Guy au Europa screamed and hit a switch on his control panel. Steam screamed from the coffin, gusting out into the already humid haze of the den. Kcaz coughed, sweeping his arm to clear the mist.

A gun barrel was shoved in Kcaz's face, an unrecognizable heavy caliber weapon with a line of glowing blue coils. *Well, found the anti-armour.* Kcaz jerked to the side as an explosion of burning metal erupted above his head. Nearby terminals went down. Hackers screamed and shouted.

When the steam cleared, Guy au Europa was gone. Kcaz hissed and ran toward the lift. He caught Guy's scent, body odour and burnt coffee.

He saw the skeletal figure at the lift, hitting the button repeatedly.

Kcaz roared, "Hold it!"

When the lift chimed open, Guy threw back an arm and fired recklessly. The recoil knocked him back. Another computer terminal exploded into bits of plastic and wiring. Kcaz could feel the heat from the slag through his suit, but he didn't lose a step. He slammed into the lift doors just as they were shutting.

"Fucker." He dug his claws into the gap. His chest heaved beneath his shirt, his bulging arms threatening to rip the sleeves. The mechanism shuddered and the doors flew open. Kcaz threw himself against the wall of the lift shaft. He scrambled up to the next level using the cabling.

Sweat pooled beneath Kcaz's clothes as he climbed. He launched himself at the third level door, digging one hand into the gap while the other gripped a piston girder.

An explosion boomed from up above. The lift came hurtling down the shaft.

SHIT.

He forced himself onto the third floor, yanking his feet away just before the lift could sheer him off the side of the shaft. It crashed below.

Kcaz grunted, rolling onto his front. He scrambled back into pursuit. Guy would be fleeing the spire.

The huge orc sprinted through a small CorpFirm floor, heedless of the lines of cubicles filled with bored looking humans and goblins. Kcaz crashed into a clerk, knocking their papers up into the air and onto the floor. He continued running.

He burst into a stairwell. He could hear footsteps echoing from up above.

Got you.

Kcaz pursued the suspect up another three flights of stairs, then heard another door slam open. Kcaz pushed harder, his legs burning with each flight. He couldn't lie, it felt good to be on the hunt again. That was exactly what scared him.

He ran through the door and into a busy tunnel connecting two spires. There were a few shops set into the bedrock. A window that ran the length of the floor showed how much higher these people were from the ones below them. Guy was visible through the flowing crowd, a skeleton as pale as milk.

Guy fired another reckless shot, blowing out the light right above Kcaz. Sparks fell down on the orc's shoulders. People in the crowd screamed and fled in all directions.

He's a fucking public danger.

Someone screamed for the district police. Kcaz drew his RC 1919, the heavy barrel trained on the fleeing hacker.

There was piping along the walls.

Kcaz closed one eye, exhaled, and pulled the trigger.

The pipes erupted in a geyser of hot steam, knocking Guy au Europa off his feet and into the other wall.

Kcaz was on him with three bounding steps.

"I got some questions for you," growled the orc, spit flying off his fangs. He picked up the weapon Guy had used, a handheld anti-armour cannon with a boxy chamber and textured grip. The damage it had caused smelled the exact same as the raid site in the Eleventh. "Where did you get this?"

◆

"What the fuck did you think you were doing?" hissed the police lieutenant.

Kcaz sat chained to the desk, glaring back. "I don't see my lawyer."

"Godamnit, Kcaz," said Lieutenant Baldr, "we're on the same side. I got the call from the Eleventh. We all want to find the culprits."

"Then why am I still here?"

Lieutenant Baldr was a small Eastlander man. He had blonde hair, blue eyes, and a vaguely dwarvish appearance. His uniform fit nicely, at least. "Come on, Kcaz! You know the game. Just tell me what the hell was going on in there."

Kcaz knew Baldr. Human police lieutenant in an orc

dominated district was a tough job. They had done some cases together in the past. Didn't mean this case would be as mutually agreeable.

"Nah," said Kcaz. "What you want is to find them yourself and garner the rewards, while *I* get to be next on the chopping block. I think not."

"Perceptive as always."

"Then let me go, Baldr," hissed Kcaz. "You know you aren't going to get anything from me, and you're not going to tell me anything either. Let bygones be bygones."

"Perhaps. You ever wonder why the Clans have us chasing our tails?" said Balder, stroking his beard. "Police find the thugs, you find the mastermind. Have us all competing for their approval."

Kcaz stared at him flatly. "I really don't have time for the philosophy lecture."

"I thought you liked a good story."

"I like when ignorant fools let me go."

"Then I'll make it easy for you," said Baldr. "Tell me what Guy au Europa told you and I'll let you go. Don't, and you can enjoy a stint downtown for a few days while we find the mastermind. I get points with the Eleventh's police department, you get to go free."

"Ask him yourself."

"*He* has a good lawyer and is already out."

"You're kidding me."

"He has a *very* good lawyer. You're lucky he's not pressing charges for the burns he sustained."

Piece of shit— Kcaz glanced at the two-way mirror, his options collapsing in on themselves. He needed this case. More importantly, *he* needed to solve it; otherwise his ass would be on the DarkHart's hit list. He didn't need goblin assassins at his door. He had enough problems. Kcaz narrowed his hazel eyes. Guy au Europa lawyering up and running meant he was guilty of something, but not necessarily a connection to the convoy raid.

Kcaz sighed, knowing that giving up the info might help in the long run. "Lizza of Dunwich." The one name Guy au Europa gave before the police arrested them both.

"What?"

"That's what he said. I was hunting for anyone with heavy weaponry ties. When I asked, Guy pulled the anti-armour on me. He said Lizza of Dunwich sold him the weapon. Seller may know who armed the orcs in the eleventh."

"You're shitting me." Baldr looked offended, like Kcaz was doing a bad job of lying. Worst part, he wasn't.

"What?"

"That's all he said?"

"Yeah," said Kcaz. "Lizza of Dunwich sold him the anti-armour. Or at least that's what he said."

"He's a lying bastard then." Baldr reached over and unlocked the manacles that enclosed Kcaz's wrists. Kcaz pulled them free, working the feeling back into his muscles. "Get out, Kcaz. I'll make sure the Chief knows you've hit a dead end. I'm sure the DarkHarts will appreciate that."

"Fuck's your problem?" hissed Kcaz. "They got your balls in a vice?"

"No, they got eyes on my daughters if I don't behave." Baldr got up to leave. "You'll be surprised to learn that Lizza of Dunwich, born Eliza Fisher, is dead. She died last year in a car crash. Was a big scandal for those who cared about it." The door slammed shut behind him.

♦

Kcaz returned to his office-apartment before midnight. He was absolutely exhausted, barely standing. *How many hours has it been now?* He flipped on the radio, and poured himself a cold, sad cup of coffee. He collapsed into his chair, fighting to stay awake while he slowly sipped his drink.

A low bass riff and a whining sax cried over the radio.

Kcaz opened the bottom desk drawer, staring at the bottle of whiskey for a long moment. His pointed ears twitched. A ghost of a memory played in his brain. A battle between petty warlords of Cascadia. Gunfire, explosions, blood, and screams.

Kcaz growled and shut the drawer. *Nothing more embarrassing than an orc with PTSD.* Most orcs had a Clan to help them through it. Community and responsibility covered the difference; the damage could be repaired, or at least handled, as a group. But Kcaz was alone.

He opened his laptop and searched for anything on Lizza of Dunwich and her connection to anti-armour weapon sales.

◆

The weapons used in the convoy raid and by Guy au Europa were URG 18s—railguns. They used a coil of electron powered magnets to fire metal filament particles at incredible speeds. It was sophisticated weaponry, hard to build, but there were thousands of adequate gunsmiths across the Underground. *Follow the seller, not the maker.* Whoever had given the weapons to the orc thieves had also given one of them to Guy au Europa, but whether it was in payment or for use in a separate crime still remained to be seen.

On the other hand, why had Guy au Europa said Lizza of Dunwich gave it to him? When could she have done so?

The weapon had been taken by the police as evidence. Kcaz wouldn't be able to track manufacturing, age, or other details now. *It's all just so circumstantial*, thought Kcaz. *Guy could have nothing to do with any of this.*

He felt drawn to the name Lizza of Dunwich, however, and she was certainly dead.

Kcaz always held heavy suspicion towards those who *died* in the Underground. If one paid the right technician, surgeon, or even magician; they could get a new face and a new life. Faking one's death was equally convenient for the right price.

But this was different. "She really is dead…"

Multiple doctors had confirmed her death due to the numerous inquiries from the NeoAnglia Embassy. *Which means she was no exiled daughter.* She had concerned people back home. His eyes drifted eastward. The proverbial ocean of the Right Side's Midwest divided the continent in half—across the Veil it was a thousand miles of farmland, but on the Wrong Side it was tiny avenues of travelable wilderness dotted with Exposed communities. The Right Side resisted the touch of the Wrong Side. On the far side of that maze lay NeoAnglia, a land of mists and moors along the rugged Atlantic coast.

Lizza was an asset and a valued member of her family, a well-to-do Anglo house. Her featured articles in the feeds and CorpFirm records meant she was doing business here and sending money back home. *A daughter sent to spread Anglo influence.* She was an instrument of soft-power-warfare between nations.

"Then why did the hacker drop her name?" Kcaz said, to himself. It was nearly four in the morning. He had had zero sleep and had already emptied another two pots of coffee. The radio hummed an upbeat swing tune.

Kcaz rubbed his eyes. He needed sleep. He checked his emails and saw the flagged messages from the phone company and the bank. He owed money. He had none. With the Blue Orchid case reaching a dead end, Kcaz had to find the convoy mastermind. He needed the pay. The Clan pay would hold him over a few months.

"Come on," said Kcaz. "What's someone like that have? Friends? Maybe. Maybe they could confirm who she was talking to before she died? Maybe the raid was set up before she died?"

Everything is a fucking maybe. Kcaz needed some certainty. He picked up his landline. The phone rang three times before a low Anglo accent drawled through the receiver.

"NeoAnglian consulate..."

♦

Kcaz ended up in the Third District for his meeting with one of Lizza's associates. The Third District was the beating heart of economic power in the Underground. The First District belonged to the KingClan, the Second to the warlike RedClan, and the Third to the banking tribe, the SilverClan.

Spires and towers rose up around the courtyard. CorpLords, clerks, adepts, lawyers, technicians, nobles, dukes, lords, and bosses of every rank and file streamed past Kcaz in a churning sea of suits, hats, and phone calls. The avenue was narrow, the gothic-inspired buildings on either side rising up to the cavern's vaulted ceilings. There were billions of credits flooding through the sparkling towers. There were a ton of stock exchange battles taking places across the trading floors, thousands of brokers waging wars for their overlords.

Through the swirling chaos came a small clerk. She bumbled through the crowd like a newborn foal, constantly bumping into people and apologizing. Her name was Demi Oncraft. A clerk in the NeoAnglia embassy.

Kcaz turned from the coffee stand, a tall latte pinched between his claws.

The girl rushed forward. "I'm so sorry I'm late. I got held up at—"

"It's fine." Kcaz shook the small human's hand before taking her to go buy her a hot dog.

They found a bench in a courtyard away from any cameras. Demi would only meet in public, but that didn't mean Kcaz was going to flaunt his face to the numerous cameras.

The courtyard centered on a statue commemorating a major SilverClan Boss. The richly dressed captain stood over a broken anvil with an arm full of tallies and purses. It was an ugly little thing, and Kcaz's disgust only grew worse the longer he looked at it.

Demi ate her veggie dog slowly. Kcaz noticed that she smelled of pine and clove—NeoAnglian perfume. His predatory instincts filed the smell away.

"You were asking about Lizza?" asked Demi.

"Yeah." Kcaz flipped through his notes on his phone. "She really is dead, yeah?"

Demi looked up, brow furrowed and lips thin. "Of course she is! What kind of question is that?!"

Kcaz frowned. "People fake things all the time here. Pop over to a talented magician and you can have a new face. I just need to make sure."

"She is!" snapped Demi, her eyes glistening. Kcaz had struck a nerve.

Kcaz's ears drooped. "My apologies, miss. I meant no offence."

"It's fine…" She took another bite of her veggie dog. "I've only been in the Underground for two years. I'm not up to snuff on everything."

"How's the UV withdrawal?"

She looked up, reading Kcaz's grim face. "Fucking awful. I go to salons, but it's getting expensive going every week. Some days I just sit under a UV lamp for hours."

"The headaches too?"

"Yeah," said Demi. "The Medica put me on supplements. The consulate takes care of us, but—"

"It's not the same. It's hard just accepting life without the sun."

"How long have you been here?"

"Pretty much always. Born outside, but I come and go. I've been back for almost a year. I was out for almost seven, but it ended badly. Had nowhere else to go but come back."

"You were born here?"

"No," said Kcaz. "But this is all I know." He looked up at the gothic buttresses and spiraling towers. He twirled his phone between his hands. His mouth watered for a drink of ale. He couldn't help but remember the bad things that had happened outside the Underground.

Demi exhaled. She seemed to relax, giving that slice of what Kcaz was looking for. "Lizza didn't do anything illegal."

"How did you know each other?"

Demi tossed her veggie dog into the trash can. "My mom was her wet nurse in NeoAnglia. I was a member of her family's household from the time I could walk. The patronage helped us move away from the low Dunwich wards and helped me get an education. Then Lizza brought me with her when she moved here. We were friends." She said the word friends with more meaning than most humans did. There was clearly more to it than Demi was lettingon. The girl was bad at hiding secrets.

"Go on," said Kcaz.

"Lizza never did anything illegal, but she had *associates*. We introduced people, helped them make deals. She kept her hands clean, but certainly benefited from some stuff she never talked about. Sometimes she was an intermediary between people."

"That's still criminal if it's against the Clans."

"But..." she looked at Kcaz. "Fine. I don't know who could possibly connect Lizza to this. Try Casey Chiba. They didn't do business, but they were close." Her eyes were watery, as if she wanted to cry.

Kcaz kept his face from dropping like a brick. "Thanks." He stood up, brushing himself off, trying to look casual. He looked down at the mousy clerk.

Kcaz scribbled an address on a notepad and tore it off for the girl. "On really bad days, go here. Don't mention my name. The password is 'Pythia Apollo'."

She took the note and read it quickly. "Thank you."

Kcaz carried on through the labyrinth of the Underground. He wasn't entirely sure that Lizza of Dunwich was the thread he should be following, but the trail seemed to indicate her involvement. If she had been an intermediary between players, then Guy's dropping of her name made sense. If someone had worked through Lizza to fund the convoy raid, then she was the link connecting the mastermind to the crime. Kcaz took the subway to the Fourth District and got a cubicle in a computer den. He was surrounded by swimmers immersed within the jungle of cables and screens. The perfumed haze and whirling cooling fans swirled the stagnant air around him. The sounds of chirping, electronic bleating, and video game gunfire filled the hall. Kcaz fought through his exhaustion with a bowl of noodles served by the den's kitchen.

A chill crawled up his spine due to one name. Casey Chiba. He searched her up through the police database and media feeds.

She was an independent contractor for the RedClan, a bounty hunter, a hacker, a cowboy— a street samurai for all intents and purposes. The new kind of mercenary that grew out of the swimmer dens, but the ones who didn't get lost in cyberspace. They were the ones who knew how to use it to their advantage.

She had had several scandals with various major Goblin Clans and other UpTown notables. Thefts, sex tapes, hacking controversies, and jobs gone badly. Kcaz saw her mugshot from her last stint in a DownTown prison ward.

Twenty-seven, Nipponi, five-foot-seven. Born in the 25th District's lowest wards. A hatchet job of scars across her narrow face; short black hair streaked with blue arranged to hide most of the damage. Her furious glare set with wolfish eyes. According to the feeds and chatrooms,

Chiba was a precise killer.

It was too good to be true. She was the perfect candidate to have masterminded a theft like the convoy raid, she even had her fingers in advanced weaponry sales. The exact sort of person Kcaz was searching for: dangerous and brilliant, with exactly the expertise and connections that could pull a heist like that off. It put his teeth on edge. It was *too* perfect a fit.

Chiba was, by reputation, pragmatic. She would be reasonable to speak to...at least Kcaz hoped so.

Kcaz's phone buzzed. He picked it up. "It's Kcaz."

An automated voice answered. "Greetings, Kcaz Skry, this is Samantha Mae McCarthy of the Central District attorney office, I would like to notify you—" Kcaz slammed the button.

"Fuck you, Samantha Mae McCarthy!"

Kcaz's phone buzzed again. He picked it up. "What?"

"Hi! Listen, it's Cadus. We gotta talk. We—"

Kcaz cut him off. "You secured this line?"

Cadus paused before he said, "Yeah."

Idiot. Kcaz could taste the lie through the receiver. "I'll be in the Eleventh in an hour. Know the coffee shop on Fjord-7?"

"Yeah."

"Good." He ended the call.

♦

The shop was a closet-sized space that wafted coffee and savoury kebab smells onto the street. The narrow alley of the District's MidTown flashed with neon signs from a dozen other eateries. Along the streets were gangs of street urchins, hulking creatures passing by, and abhumans— the old gothic for non-human humanoids—smoking and complaining in groups.

Kcaz entered the shop, a quiet retreat from the buzz of the activity outside. The hostess, Mira, squealed his name. She was a girl with coppery skin and a black braid. She took Kcaz's claw into her soft hands. "What are you doing here?!"

"Business, sadly. There's a pig here. Seen him?"

"Back corner."

Kcaz floated through the cramped shop. He swerved around the server, Mona. She gave him a wide smile.

Officer Cadus sat alone at a table. The Carib-born man nursed a coffee. He had heavy bags under his eyes. *Gods, does anyone get any sleep around here?* Kcaz slipped into the chair. Mona brought him a coffee, pouring the black liquid in a long waterfall-like pour. Steam rose around

Kcaz's gargoyle-like face.

"Thank you, Mona," said Kcaz as she floated away.

A silence hung between Kcaz and Cadus, two exhausted agents of the establishment. The restaurant continued to bustle around them, traditional music crackled over a radio.

"You alright, Kcaz?"

"Fine." Kcaz sipped his coffee. "Good hunting?"

"You could say that."

"Then what the fuck am I doing here? Or should I expect a red dot over my shoulder?"

Cadus looked insulted, ass if such tactics were beneath him. *They never were.* Morals and codes were cheap in the Underground, especially for District Police. They always were.

"No," said Cadus. "I just needed to tell you something. We caught two of the boys involved in the raid."

Kcaz's brow furrowed. He knew there was more. He could smell the fear on Cadus. He had pheromone levels that would send a wild orc into a predatory killing spree. Kcaz saw it on Cadus's face, in the dilation of his eyes and the nervous tick in his lip.

"We found two boys," said Cadus. "Sixteen years old. Kids"

"Adults. I was full grown at twelve." Now Kcaz was nearly forty, as old as many successful warlords. "Outcasts?"

"Seems like," said Cadus, sipping his coffee. "Perfect for a job against the Clans."

"Too perfect…"

"Yeah," said Cadus. He leaned forward. "We found them with scraps of stamped platinum. They were drunk. We processed them and threw them into interrogation for a few hours."

Kcaz's ears drooped. The officer was terrified. Kcaz leaned forward before Cadus spoke again.

"Both were dead when I got back. Knife across the throat. Blood everywhere."

Kcaz leaned back, letting the information settle over him. "No one saw it?"

"Not a thing," said Cadus. "Recordings were erased. They must've hacked it. We have absolutely nothing to go on."

"Yeah, you do," said Kcaz. He called Mona over and ordered a kebab. He suddenly felt very hungry. "It means someone powerful backed the raid and they know they're being investigated. It means they have ears in your precinct, and it means they'll kill you to keep the Clans from finding out."

Means they'll be after me too.

Cadus understood the last part. He was trembling. It wasn't just Kcaz who was waiting for that red dot to appear on his forehead.

Kcaz's food came. He ate the kebab in one bite. "I recommend taking a few days off. Find a motel in the Twenty-first District. Some place awful, a real pit, somewhere you won't relax. Give me a few days and I'll sort it out."

"You have a lead?"

"I ain't telling you a damn thing." Kcaz shovelled the side of berber rice into his jaws. "If they catch you, they'll know. Thanks for the lunch."

Kcaz got up to leave, giving smiles and nods to the staff as he left.

♦

Stay awake, old boy, thought Kcaz. *Stay awake.* He shook his head like a bear shaking off fleas. A headache had begun to come on, made worse by the ward he had just entered.

Kcaz stalked down the sidewalk of Okar Ward, Sixth

District. Neon light cascaded around him in a torrent. Music boomed, voices howled, and the ebb and flow of party goers swirled around him. In his charcoal suit and coat, Kcaz was a dark pillar in the multi-coloured crowd. Glowing paint turned goblins into gods, elves into demons, and humans into monsters. Spires of neon and chrome rose up over the boardwalk. Projections of dancers, courtesans, and dragons danced across the dazzling structures.

With no day and night cycle, the measure of time became less meaningful. There were no weekends or weekdays, just constant cycles of shifts and time off. As a result, the pleasure wards that populated every district were round-the-clock parties. This one was in the upper reaches of the Sixth District. It was a frequent haunt of Casey Chiba.

A staircase led to a den under the street. The neon sign of a storm demon floated overhead. Kcaz was stepping into a wolf den. He wished he had the option to search for evidence from a distance. *Find information on the net. Talk to Chiba's associates. Get data on her somehow.* He had wanted to avoid a direct confrontation with Chiba, but she kept her associates close, select, and often under watch.

She was a professional, but far from a quiet pawn in the clan's games.

Please let her be reasonable... Kcaz had had his fill of

the lunatics that filled the Underground.

Kcaz descended the steps into the den and knocked on a door. After a brief pause, a robotic eye on an arm popped out of the wall. It studied Kcaz, blinking and dilating its optics.

"Business?"

Kcaz held up his identification.

There was another pause before the eye retracted itself back into the wall. The door didn't open. Kcaz knocked on the door again. Nothing. Then he slammed his fist on the panel. Kcaz stretched his back, loosening his muscles. He didn't want to have to open the door by force. As he began to judge how best to crack it open, the locking mechanism shuddered. The door swung open, and Kcaz entered the wolf den.

Three syndicate thugs waited inside, glowing tattoos of dragons and wolves over their arms and chests. One had a bionic eye with wiring sprouting from his temple. Another held a pistol, red chrome with a narrow barrel. They all carried straight-backed katanas on their belts.

They searched Kcaz up and down before taking his firearm.

"This way," grunted the one with the bionic eye.

Kcaz followed the foot soldier down a spiralling staircase. The stairs led down into the bedrock of the mountain. The walls were lined with pipes and a ribbon of low blue lights. Chambers split off from the central spiral, the dens of syndicate bosses, their sons, and servants. Casey Chiba was just another samurai lost in the endless feuds, duels, and political maneuverings that the Underground thrived on. *One day they'd all be eaten by the mountains too. Like Nyrvellir; like a thousand other would-be overlords.*

They eventually came to a den, the door flanked by two more samurai. One wore a wolfish battle mask. They bowed and bid Kcaz enter.

He gritted his fangs, feeling he was stepping into an unholy sanctum.

Inside, the apartment was dark. It had low blue lighting, a living room with black leather furniture, and a widescreen displaying the recent football matches.

Chiba sat at the table, tapping at a dataslate. At her side was an attendant, a samurai with her hair in a bun.

Chiba looked up from the dataslate with her yellow, wolfish eyes. She narrowed them at the gigantic orc that had entered her domain. If she was surprised, she didn't show it. She was smaller than Kcaz felt she should be—a scorpion in its nest.

Chiba wore a low-cut t-shirt under her leather jacket, her red steel-capped boots were set on the coffee table. A ribbon of smoke rose from an ashtray by her feet.

Chiba clicked her tongue and the woman rushed out; perfume evaporated with the scent of fear. The door closed behind Kcaz, trapping him alone in the room with the street samurai.

"Kcaz Skry," said Chiba. "How unexpected."

Kcaz kept his face neutral. "You know me?"

"I know of you. I know every agent of the Clans across the Underground," she sipped whiskey from a crystal glass. "To what do I owe the pleasure?"

"Work, I'm afraid."

Chiba continued her perfect poker face. Kcaz couldn't smell the faintest hint of fear on her; she was in complete control.

"Please sit," said Chiba. She poured a second glass of whiskey for Kcaz, but he didn't touch it.

Kcaz sat. Chiba was tall for a human woman, but she would barely come up to Kcaz's chest at his full height. Even so, he knew that this was far more dangerous than anything he'd done in months. The woman's face was a mess of hatchet scars, her black-blue hair arranged to help hide part of it, and her wolfish eyes were intense.

"So, tell me, what have I been accused of this time?"

"Not a thing," said Kcaz. He let the implicit yet left unsaid. "But I'll get to the point. Did you kill Lizza of Dunwich?"

Chiba coughed on her cigarette. She brushed ashes off her shirt, recomposing herself.

Gotcha, thought Kcaz.

The woman studied Kcaz for a moment before speaking. "Of course not. The police already confirmed her death to satisfy inquiries from NeoAnglia.Over a year ago. Why the hell are you investigating it now?"

"So, you were well acquainted?"

Her yellow eyes narrowed. "You're a bad liar, Mr. Skry. Cut the bullshit. I don't have time for an orc with too many questions."

Kcaz chuckled. "Just testing the waters, my lady."

"I'm not a lady."

"Manners. Apologies."

"This isn't some UpTown court. What the hell do you want?"

"You heard about the raid in the Eleventh? A bunch of

Clan platinum went missing."

"I heard," said Chiba. "I also heard that the culprits have been dropping like flies in police custody." She sipped her whiskey. "Please have a drink."

Kcaz flipped through his notes, ignoring the invitation. "Where'd you hear about that?"

"Please, Mr. Skry. It's my job to know. Get to the point."

"That *is* the point. I am following up on suspicions that you may be involved."

Her face remained neutral.

"How familiar are you with anti-armour weapons trade?"

Chiba remained unmoved.

"Did you or any of your men have anything to do with the raid on the Clans' platinum?"

She looked insulted. "My men aren't stupid enough to steal from the Clans."

"Oh, but *you* are. You've done it three times."

She burst out laughing. "Yes, but I didn't raid a DownTown convoy. What kind of fucking moron would do something like that? There are plenty of easier and more effective ways to steal from the Clans."

"Exactly what I thought," said Kcaz. "But given your associations with Lizza of Dunwich, a name that has come up in my investigation, it makes me wonder if you supplied the anti-armour weapons."

"I did no such thing." The samurai was getting angry. Her scowl flexed the scars.

"Not like you would tell me," said Kcaz. "But I do need to find where those boys got the anti-armour. Given your history with the Clans and your connections with black market weapons, I had to follow up."

Chiba's glare was like daggers. "Please, have a drink."

He ignored the request.

"No one comes to mind? No mutual associates?"

Chiba remained unmoved. Kcaz played the only card he had left.

He stood up. "Have a pleasant day, Miss Chiba."

He'd only made it halfway to the door when she hissed, "Try Boss Dekar Invad of the HardFists. He trades the same weapons used in the raids, or he used to."

"Used to?"

"Then he found politics." She tapped her dataslate and the door slid open. "See yourself out, Skry. I have work to do. Please, take the drink with you."

"Sorry, alcohol doesn't agree with me."

"That's not what I gathered," said Chiba. "Last I heard you were a drunken mercenary who would commit any crime in the book for a fifth of whiskey." She took the glass she had poured for Kcaz and downed the amber liquid herself. "I heard you ran with some upstart from the Twenty-fourth District. Some warlord-prince with green eyes."

Kcaz felt a rush of adrenaline in his limbs at the memories. The mistakes. *Why are we doing this, Marek?!*

Chiba smiled at his visible discomfort. "Then he got the whole roving band of killers murdered. Yet here you are, still alive, returned to the Underground to scrape by. Quite a story. No one ever told me what happened between you and him."

Kcaz looked down and saw he had crushed the notepad between his claws. He ran his tongue across his fangs, imagining the taste of whiskey on the rocks. He put the crushed paper into his breast pocket.

Chiba smiled, becoming even more wolfish. "Tit for tat, Mr. Skry. You insult me, I insult you. I had nothing to do with the raid DownTown and my relationship with Lizza was strictly personal. We never once traded merchandise. She wasn't that kind of person. Not with me. Funny, I expected more from an intelligent brute."

Kcaz watched her enjoy the torment she was throwing at him.

"Tell me," Chiba dabbed her cigarette. "Did your brother keep you drunk to go along with his plans, or did you do it to numb yourself to the crimes you committed?" She looked Kcaz up and down as if she had just won a hand of cards. He glared with his hazel eyes.

"We all have our sins, Miss Chiba. We all have our ghosts." He turned back towards the door. He had gotten what he needed. Another thread. One step closer to the source of the weapons. "At least I don't have to look at mine in the mirror."

Chiba's poker face remained immovable.

He gestured to her scars. "Was it a CycleGang with a new toy? Or a CorpLord taking an urchin off the streets?"

Chiba was almost amused by the comment. "You know, I find it fascinating how little orcs seem to care about or understand the violence humans commit against each other. You'll fight to the death on a whim. You'll raid and conquer for power, security, and survival. With humans, everything gets tied up in breeding. All the pain and violence is all wired in with… 'what can I fuck' and 'can I ensure what I fuck carries on my genes.'" Chiba poured herself another drink. "It's poor form to throw something like that at a lady."

"You're no lady," said Kcaz.

Chiba chuckled and shot back her whiskey. "You know I can't have someone disrespect me and walk away unpunished right? How will my men stay in line if a big dumb orc won't give me my due?"

Kcaz had hoped to avoid this. He let out a beleaguered exhale. "Was hoping you'd make an exception."

She whipped the glass at Kcaz. He ducked and it smashed against the wall. Chiba drew a katana out from behind the couch and swung for his head. Kcaz caught Chiba's wrist. She spat in his face.

"Get the fuck out of here, Skry."

Kcaz growled. "Thank you for the enlightening talk." He picked her up and threw her sideways into the widescreen. The panel shattered into a spider web of fractures.

Chiba thudded against the floor. She groaned, then picked herself up. Her yellow, wolfish eyes glared at Kcaz.

Kcaz grit his teeth. *Here we go again.*

Chiba stumbled into the hall. "Someone kill this greenie!"

Four thugs rushed into view;,their swords already drawn. Kcaz bared his teeth, an intimidating display that was all instinct. Kcaz fell into them like a lion into a pack of jackals. He roared, slamming them into the walls with bone crunching force. He caught wrists and diverted weapons into their comrades. A shot from one of the pistols burst open a thug's arm. To Kcaz, they were rag dolls, weak little men with no hope at victorious close quarters combat with a brutish orc. Bones crunched. The sound of screams spiked and then fell into groans.

Kcaz dropped the last body—the one with the bionic eye—to the floor.

Chiba glared from around the corner, clutching her bruised ribs.

"I'll see you around Chiba!" roared Kcaz.

"Fuck you, Skry!" she howled. "Be seeing you." She vanished.

Kcaz had no reason to pursue her. Kcaz suspected she knew more than she was letting on, but Chiba was a professional. She was innocent of any role in the convoy raid. She had given Kcaz something to work with. He had the name of a weapons dealer. Dekar Invad, HardFist Clan.

He brushed himself off and carried on into the Underground.

♦

Kcaz sat in the metro, waiting for his subway. He checked his watch. He didn't like the idea of Boss Dekar Invad being the culprit. It didn't hold up.

He had gone to another internet café for some cursory information and had transferred the data to his phone. He wasn now scrolling through it.

Dekar Invad, orc, Boss of the HardFist. He was one of the Tenth District's lower ward bosses, a small-time thug, and a member of the Orc Resurgence Party.

Kcaz chewed his lip when he realized what he was walking into.

Orcs across the Underground resented Goblin Clan authority. "Against the natural order of things," they would say. Across the world, orcs dominated goblins by the right of the mighty. As lions dominated their prides, orcs ruled over goblins. Not in the Underground, however, not under the umbrella of the Goblin King. Whatever failures orcs faced, they blamed it on goblin rule. Now some were organizing that into a political movement.

The subway rolled in and traded passengers. Kcaz

let himself be carried with the crowd, gripping a handle above.

Dekar was a radical, a thug with delusions of grandeur.

The subway jerked into motion, hurtling through the labyrinth of lines between districts.

It didn't make sense that someone with that kind of reputation would be assassinating the boys he hired. No. Dekar likely didn't know a thing about the raid, but he would have a good idea of where the weapons came from. That was as good a thread as anything.

Outcasts were considered vermin by most Clans, hence the runts trying to take slices off of Kcaz every other day in the Eighth. Either exiled from their own clans or they simply never had one. Clan bias against outcasts could have outweighed Dekar's political ambitions. Orcs were born—for lack of a better word—nearly full grown, with no infant or child stage. Kcaz had been five-foot-two when he crawled out of his spawning hole. He didn't remember much of his first few weeks of life; he had been alone, an outcast, forgotten. That was, until some humans found him. He had spent nearly thirty seasons outside as a mercenary.

It had been his last stretch as a mercenary that had gone badly. Worse than badly. He rubbed his eyes. Fighting to keep the memories back, he forced himself to breathe slow, deep breaths. Sleep deprivation made it harder than usual. His senses were dulled nearly to a drunken stupor. He checked the time. *Nearly four days without sleep...*

He went back to his data on Dekar. The raid on the convoy could have multiple motivations. He could dispose of some unwanted outcasts, pull a job against the Clans, and get some wealth to fund his political movement.

The subway swayed to a halt at the next station.

The synthetic voice chimed. "Next stop, Fourteenth Ward, Tenth District. Please mind the gap. Please mind the gap."

Kcaz felt a rush of air on the back of his neck and he caught the smell of metal.

His hand shot out instinctively. The knife went straight through his palm. Red-purple blood trailed down his hand to his wrist, staining his sleeve. He grunted.

The thug was a human youth wearing a hood. Kcaz wrapped his bleeding hand around the knife, slashing his claws across the human's sleeve. The young face was hidden by his cowl; they broke themselves free of the orc's grip. Kcaz was entrapped by the crowd around them, his size now a handicap.

The hooded killer rushed out of the car just as the doors began to close. Kcaz shouldered his way through the press of bodies, nearly knocking over an elderly woman. The woman's huge eyes promised a scream. Kcaz bumbled for apologies; when he looked back up it was too late.

The doors sealed shut with a hiss. The subway jerked back into motion.

Kcaz watched the hooded figure disappear into the crowds at the station. He was a small human in a baggy sweater and jeans, his sleeve was torn where Kcaz's claws had torn into his wrist, and blood dripped from his fingers.

The mastermind had just taken a shot at Kcaz, either themself or through an agent. They'd found out about Kcaz in the same way they'd learned about the outcasts being arrested. They had taken their shot and failed.

Now they knew a bit more about each other. The mastermind saw Kcaz as a threat that needed removing.

But Kcaz wouldn't be so easily taken out.

Kcaz wrapped his hand with a handkerchief to stop the bleeding. He was getting close to the culprit behind the raid. Close enough to be in danger. *I've been in danger the entire time...*If he failed to find the mastermind, the DarkHart Clan would make an example of him. They'd skin him alive. *Don't fail the clans.* That's something he had learned when he was very young. And he never had— that's why he could keep coming back to the Underground when things went bad on the outside. He shuddered.

He continued on the subway, hurtling further toward who he hoped was the true mastermind behind the raid.

◆

Kcaz arrived in the Tenth District's DownTown ward shortly after. He adjusted the handkerchief around his hand. The wound would knit in due time. If he couldn't stop for sleep then he couldn't stop for an injury.

He stood on a wide avenue in an open-air cavern. Housing blocks, corporate spires, and shopping plazas filled the cavern and climbed up its walls. Above were the lights of more roof-side structures. The ward wasn't in the best place. Currently a turf war between Dekar's HardFist Clan and a local Italian family, the Corellis, was taking place. There had been a shootout a few blocks over. The district police didn't care. LowClan scuffles weren't their problem. It was the survival of the fittest in the pits of the Underground. DownTown always felt like being in a termite nest being raided by ants.

Kcaz entered Dekar's apartment block by pressing all the keys until someone hit the buzzer. The walls were splattered with HardFist emblems and graffiti. A woman sat smoking at the bottom of the stairs. As Kcaz ascended toward Dekar's apartment, a pair of orc runts rushed up past him.

"Come on," said one. "We're gonna be late."

They didn't wear any clan icons. They were outcasts. Kcaz narrowed his eyes and followed the boys. The graffiti-splattered hallway led to the open door of a suite filled with more orcs of various sizes, all leaning in toward the apartment. The runts were forced to get up on their toes to see.

Before Kcaz reached the suite, he paused by a closed apartment door. A familiar scent played at his nose; he couldn't quite place it. He shook his head and continued down the hall.

The suite was packed with a crowd as diverse in shape and shade as the mess hall in the Eighth. The wolves, lions, boars and bears had all set aside their differences for an afternoon. They sat in still silence. Kcaz blinked twice, surprised—nearly shocked. He'd never seen anything like this before.

At the center was Boss Dekar. He was a seven-foot-tall monster with a bulbous nose, a heavy jaw, and a cracked pair of tusks. He wore a blazer and slacks. His chest of cable-like muscles rippled beneath his tank top.

"We can't keep living as divided thugs and monsters!" shouted Dekar. "Clan verses outcasts, this Clan verses that Clan, big verses small—we can't be fighting amongst ourselves while we get left out of all the decisions."

A few quiet murmurs rippled through the bestial audience.

"Brothers, we have no districts ruled by an orc clan. We have no authoritative body to represent us," said Dekar. "You know how the goblins took over the Underground? Well?" Silence from the crowd followed.

A vulture-faced runt put his hand up. "They stole it, boss."

"Exactly, lad!" roared Dekar, his voice booming. "They took it. Power must be taken. Orcs know this. Goblins know this. All the CorpLords and the kings and dukes of UpTown know this. They like to say they have rules of chivalry and honour, but we know they don't. They steal power as quick as an outcast would a loaf of bread. Tell me, who knows the history—why did the goblin clans win the Underground when all others failed?"

More silence.

"Well come on! Someone's got to have an idea?"

Kcaz sighed. He needed to talk to Dekar in private, but investigating the raid while surrounded by orcs—some of whom could very well be involved—was not a good plan. Kcaz put his hand up; he needed to move things along. "Unity."

"Aye, that's right, brother." Dekar held his long arms

out to the crowd. "The goblin clans had a level of unity previously unseen by this world. They worked *together* to take the Underground. They built their power base and for almost a century they've ruled over us like masters."

"Fascists!" barked a runt.

"Aye," said Dekar. "Let's not throw that word around. Orcs and goblins have always understood the simple truth of the world—the right of the mighty. Power decides, nothing else. Listen here, I've been reading more of the humie literature. Some of them got quite a sense of how power is built, and how it's sustained and maintained through systems of control."

Dekar then began reciting literature from first-year political theory lectures. Kcaz looked at the crowd. They were as entranced as any audience he had seen in the fighting pits, eating up each allegory about class consciousness, inequality, and power relations. It was as fascinating as it was bizarre.

Kcaz saw a reserved anger in the orcs' faces. He could see the dissonance between Dekar's intentions and what the results of his words were. Most of the assembled orcs weren't there for high-minded political unity, they were angry. Angry and dispossessed, they wanted a fight. They resented goblin rule because goblins weren't *supposed* to be in charge. It was alien. Dekar attracted them because an orc with big words and colourful prose was something to

LIES IN NEON

follow. Dekar may have had good points about the clans, their government, and the king, but Kcaz saw the poison in the room. They wanted power, not justice.

Kcaz waited by the door as the mob filtered out, hands in his pockets. Sleep gnawed at his mind.

"Can I help you, brother?"

Kcaz looked up. It was Dekar.

"You look rough. Long days?"

"And longer nights," said Kcaz. "May we speak in private?"

"Of course!" said Dekar. "We're all brothers here. Come along."

They entered a bedroom. Dekar was bigger than Kcaz, but in the close-confines, Kcaz was confident he could escape if he needed to. The room was set up as a private printing press. There were a few printers and a computer terminal. Stacks of newspapers, magazines, and pamphlets were piled against the walls. The bed was a nest-like pallet of old blankets.

Dekar sat backwards on a chair. He drew a box of cigarettes from his blazer and lit up a RedRoll. He offered Kcaz a stool. "What's your name?"

Kcaz took a seat and held up his identification. "I need

211

to ask you some questions, boss."

Dekar was crestfallen. Kcaz wasn't a new comrade looking to join, but an agent of the system. "Ask away. Regardless of your position, we're all brothers here."

"An interesting sentiment. You have a history of selling black market weapons in the district. Tell me, had any business lately?"

"No, sir. I've left that behind, trying to build a better future for all orcs."

"Tell me about your conflict with the Corelli family."

Dekar glared. "Every DownTown ward has its fights, this is just ours. Those Catholic humies have been muscling out non-humans for years, and I'm the only one fighting against it."

"By shooting up a diner?" asked Kcaz, quoting reports on the recent Corelli–HardFist violence.

Dekar almost burst out laughing. "You ought to know, sir. Look at you." He gestured to the scars on Kcaz's jaw and ear. "Mercenary work?"

"Aye," said Kcaz. "We all have our fights. I don't judge you for taking it to the local Italians, I just need you to answer me. Have you sold any URG-18s?"

"I haven't touched anything like that. I don't. The Corelli still do, but I do not. My commitment to orc political autonomy is sincere, Brother Skry." Dekar dabbed his cigarette in a bowl.

Kcaz changed his tactic. Perhaps Dekar had a role other than providing weapons. "It must be expensive fighting a gang war *and* being a political advocate. How do you pay for all this?"

"We pool our resources. Every brother contributes," said Dekar. "Don't worry, those meetings are free. We won't shake you down for credits. You want to get to the point?"

"Heard about the raid in the Eleventh?"

Dekar shrugged.

"Convoy raid, platinum stolen by a group of outcast boys. I'm trying to hunt down whoever set it all up. The boys who were arrested are being crossed off a hit list."

"Here's a question for you," Dekar took a long draw on his RedRoll, "Are you investigating this because a pack of outcasts got duped and you want to bring the mastermind to justice? Or because they stole from the clans?"

It wasn't the slap in the face that Dekar intended. Kcaz really didn't care about why the outcasts were being killed. He didn't want to care. *I still have a job to do and sometimes you have to be the bad guy.*

Kcaz didn't answer the question. There was no good answer. "So you deny any part in this?"

"Without a doubt."

"Do you know anyone who trades in anti-armour weapons?"

"I've cut all ties to that life. It's not my problem anymore."

"That doesn't mean you don't know who trades in weapons of that nature," said Kcaz. "None of your former associates have come by with offers?"

Dekar hesitated, a slight twinge in his ears.

"Come on, boss."

"Fine," said Dekar. "A few fools came by."

"Names?"

"One. Brutus Corelli."

"What happened?"

He dabbed his cigarette again. "I was a fool when I was younger. I had to find a new path when my brothers got hurt. I wound up in a prison ward." He met Kcaz's eyes. "I used to provide weapons to the Corelli. The very weapons they use against orcs and non-humans. The very things you're hunting for."

Kcaz cocked his head. "Go on."

"Brutus Corelli. He's the first son of the Corelli head, Atreus."

"Do you think the Corellis set those boys up to take the fall while they ran off with the platinum?"

"In my opinion, I'd say it's more than likely."

Kcaz appreciated Dekar's candidness. "Does the name 'Lizza of Dunwich' mean anything to you?"

The name brought out the surprise in Dekar's boorish features. "What does she have to do with this?"

"She seems to be the common thread connecting the weapons to the crime. Either she provided the thieves with them before she died, or someone is posing as her. You're absolutely sure she's dead?"

"Not all humans are bad, just most of them. Lizza never discussed weapon sales. She was a business woman. She wanted labour, assets, and cash to send home. She never touched crime. Wouldn't be able to send money back home if she confronted the status quo *too* much."

Kcaz nodded. "Well, Boss Dekar, this has been a most interesting and informative experience. I'll see myself out."

"Take care of yourself," said Dekar. "When you're

done working for the establishment, then maybe we can talk about fellowship."

"Boss, to share in the honest brevity," said Kcaz, "*you* may make many good points, but those boys you attract...they just want to rule and be in charge. They aren't interested in autonomy or representation. They want supremacy. You're playing with fire you don't understand."

Now that *did* sting Dekar like a slap in the face. Kcaz could see it all over the Boss before he left.

Kcaz walked solemnly down the hall. Could the Corellis have backed the raid? They had motivation for obtaining wealth and removing some local orcs. Give them a job, kill them, and reap all the benefits; it was a common tactic used by humans. *Divide and conquer.* He ground his fangs. He needed proof.

His nose flared, like a bloodhound catching a scent. He stopped in front of the apartment door he had passed when he first arrived; that familiar scent was playing with his brain, trying to remind him of something. Something was off. He leaned against the door, listening, but heard nothing.

Kcaz glanced both ways down the hall before breaking the lock. He rushed in, drawing his RC 1919. It was an empty apartment suite. All the furniture was covered in sheets. Kcaz smelled the air. It was stale with dust, but with the hint of something else.

He followed the scent, nostrils flaring. He entered the bedroom, sweeping from corner to corner with his RC-1919. After the subway, he refused to be caught defenseless. The smell grew stronger. Kcaz lowered himself to the floor and took in the smell. *Pine and clove.*

Kcaz looked up. There was an air duct above the bed. Kcaz climbed onto the bed, the mattress squeaking under his weight. He opened up the air duct, but found nothing except more dust. *I'm wasting my fucking time.*

"He's a fucking pig's pet. Lower than them—" echoed a voice through the ductwork.

Kcaz paused and listened, straining his senses. Dekar's voice drifted in through the duct, along with that of another orc. They were talking shit about Kcaz, which he expected. *But someone could listen to all his meetings.* Including the Correlli Family. They could glean information on weapons, contracts, and unemployed outcasts.

Despite Dekar's high-minded ideals, most orcs would jump at any job offer. Some certainly had in this case, and now they were all dead.

Kcaz ran back to Dekar's suite. He slammed his fist on the apartment, knocking several times in quick succession. The door opened and Dekar loomed over Kcaz.

"Who lived in the one next door to you?"

"I…no one lives there," said Dekar. "I tried to get the owners to sell it, but they said someone keeps paying for it. So, it sits empty."

Kcaz ran off, leaving the boss with a very confused look.

♦

The doors of the speakeasy burst open. Two thugs collapsed unconscious on the floor. Guns rattled from their holsters. Rogues and gangsters of the Corelli family aimed their weapons at the huge orc in the doorway.

They all thought it was another raid from the HardFist Clan, but the hulking orc was alone. Alone and wearing a crisp suit and hat. No orc in the District dressed so well.

Kcaz dipped his hat. "Here to speak to Brutus Corelli."

"For what?" hissed a man at the bar, his revolver pointed at the orc.

Kcaz sauntered further into the den. The gangsters spread out around him, wolves circling a lion. He placed his identification on the bar top. The bartender had brandished a shotgun and had it trained on Kcaz's head. The gangster eyed the orc up and down. "What do you want?"

"I need to speak to Brutus."

"You are," said the gangster. Brutus was young, maybe twenty-five, with a handsome pale face covered in scruff. He was square-jawed with a hint of baby fat, and had brown eyes shaded beneath his hat.

Kcaz leaned on the bar. "I'm low on sleep, low on coffee, and I've already been stabbed today, so I'll make it quick. You sold any URG- 18s lately?"

Brutus laughed, and the weapons surrounding Kcaz were lowered. "What? Am I under arrest for suspicion of making a buck?"

"Is that a yes?"

"No," said Brutus. "It means it ain't any of your business, greenie. Fuck off. We got a war to win with you brutes."

"No," boomed a voice from the back. "Answer him."

A tall figure stood in the doorway of the kitchen, a middle-aged man with his sleeves rolled up, his vest fronted with a splattered apron. The light behind him invaded the darkened speakeasy. "Brutus, bring our guest into the back."

Brutus sneered and obeyed, leading Kcaz into the kitchen. The bright lights revealed the man's obvious similarity to his son.

"Atreus Corelli, I presume?"

The kitchen was simple. It had a concrete floor, metal walls, a set of stoves, fryers, and a heavy wooden table. Atreus went back to the table, working pasta dough. A young girl sat at the end of the table with a binder, busy with homework. Her dark brown eyes studied the group like those of a bored student in class.

"Go on," said Atreus, working the dough. He seemed to enjoy the motion. He had the same handsome features as his son, but where Brutus had baby fat, Atreus was gaunt. Kcaz could tell he had been fighting for a long time. He could read it on his arms, his neck, and his face.

"There's nothing to say, Dad," said Brutus.

"Oh, I think there is. You said you sold them, and gave me a portion. Never a big deal, we do it weekly, but *now* we have a detective paying us a visit." Atreus's quiet calm was as terrifying as a sleeping dragon. Kcaz watched, taking in each detail. He now knew the Corellis had had no hands in the convoy raid. Atreus rolled out the dough into a paper-thin sheet. "So who did you sell the guns to?"

"A nobody," said Brutus.

Atreus looked up. "And now this nobody has done what, dear sir?"

Kcaz removed his hat. "They backed a raid in the

Eleventh and paid orc outcasts to steal millions worth of clan platinum. I need to find the one who planned it."

"So tell him, Brutus," said Atreus. "Who planned this raid?"

"I…" Brutus looked like a child about to get a spanking. Kcaz could smell the fear on him. The girl at the table wore a slight smile, evidently finding the exchange between father and son humorous. "I don't know."

Atreus stopped rolling and got out a pizza slicer. He raised an eyebrow.

"It was done through a mutual aid. Guy au Europa. Eighth District hacker."

Kcaz smiled. "Ah, yes, he had one of the URGs too. I wondered if the perp paid him with it."

"I don't know who did it. I didn't interact with them directly. It was just a weapon sale like a thousand others."

Atreus sliced the pasta with mechanical precision. His voice calm, he said, "You didn't do a background check? You didn't bother to investigate *who* we were trading with or *what* they might use the weapons for?"

"You didn't ask! You just nodded and took the money!"

Atreus finished a cut. The razor-sharp disk rang,

spinning in circles. "Mister...?"

"Skry," said Kcaz.

"Mr. Skry. I apologize for the trouble we've become entangled in. I trust you'll inform the clans of our cooperation and assure them that the culprit will be punished accordingly. We'll gladly reconfirm our subservience to the clans if necessary."

"Yes, don," said Kcaz.

"Wait—what?!" squealed Brutus.

"Hush."

Two gangsters stood in the shadows of the kitchen, watching like hounds ready to be unleashed. Atreus wiped his hands on his apron and extended a hand to Kcaz. The orc shook it.

"I'm your son!" pleaded Brutus as he was dragged out the back door.

"Yes," said Atreus, eyes not moving from Kcaz. "Which means you won't be irreparably hurt. But the clans need to know where our loyalty lies." He finally looked at his son, then at the girl at the table. "Be careful boys, he *is* my son."

Brutus's screams were audible even from the back alley.

Kcaz let go of the don's hand and left. His brain

wandered to the foreign concepts of family and clan. Kcaz had been forced to build his own on the outside. *And that blew up in my face...*

He had almost all of the pieces. The hacker had facilitated the business between players, but he wasn't the mastermind, Kcaz knew as much. Neither was Chiba...but then what had led Kcaz to her? The connection to Lizza of Dunwich, a dead expat. She had been someone who made business connections but never went against the clans. Kcaz walked toward the nearest metro station.

There was one other person who had all of Lizza of Dunwich's connections. One other person who could have organized the raid. All Kcaz had to do was prove that she had.

♦

"Ah, yes, Mr. Skry," said an automatic voice. "Your friend has been here for an hour. She is enjoying a full UV bath with a lime martini."

Kcaz closed the phone. Who was the person who had all of Lizza of Dunwich's contacts? Who knew exactly which criminal elements to maneuver around in order to set this up? Who could have appeared innocuous amongst all these hardened criminals and monsters? Who could have walked through a police department without raising an alarm? Only one person. And if they had paid Guy au

Europa to hack the cameras, then it all fit perfectly.

Demi Oncraft had taken Kcaz's advice and went to the Apollonian Club, a salon designed to help outsiders handle the problems associated with sunlight deprivation. Public UV lamps had been set up in the Underground in the reforms back in the 80s, but private salons were still common.

And who had sent Kcaz to Casey Chiba, likely hoping that all suspicion would fall on her? It had been a perfect false lead, and Kcaz had fallen for it.

He had gotten lucky. Chiba had gotten him back onto the right track.

Dekar's apartment was a treasure trove of information, and Demi had exploited the hell out of it. *Who would have suspected a tiny Anglo girl, the daughter of a wet nurse?* She would have known of Dekar through Lizza, would have been familiar with his politics, his social movement...and with the likelihood of desperate orcs showing up to follow him. Eavesdropping on his meetings and discovering the old connection with the Corellis opened the door for the weapon sale. That knowledge, combined with a bundle of URG-18s, gave her all the resources required to put her plan into action.

Kcaz walked down the darkened halls of the apartment block. The Third District's DownTown was nicer than most districts' MidTowns. It had clean hallways without graffiti or loitering creatures. Most of the tenets were goblins or humans. Demi Oncraft was a clerk in the NeoAnglia Embassy, she wasn't living in the poverty that cursed most of the Underground.

Kcaz reached her apartment. There was a computerized lock on the door. Kcaz growled. He reached for his phone. Most places he could get into by breaking down a door, but not this one. He didn't have the time, and he didn't want to attract attention. If word got out, Demi would run, disappear, sell the platinum in pieces, and vanish into the labyrinth of the Underground.

He used his claws to open the panel, then rewired the circuits to his phone. Using a program he had stolen about six months prior, he hacked the lock. The lock clicked. The door slid open without a sound.

Kcaz hid his slapdash hack job and entered the apartment.

The smell of pine and clove was strong inside the shoebox-sized apartment. There was a bed, half kitchen, and a work desk in one cell; a line of books and a computer sat on the desk. The window looked out over a deep casym in the district, the two walls covered in barnacle-like apartment blocks and shopping strips. Lights from a thousand neon signs and dancing projections bled through the blinds. *This is nicer than my entire apartment block.*

Kcaz sniffed. The scent matched the perfume he'd caught in the apartment next to Dekar's. Though his own apartment was bigger, this one didn't reek of refuse. And it didn't echo with howls from the fights down the street. The landlord likely didn't forget to repair the power or the plumbing, or ignore the requests from tenants altogether.

Kcaz smelled something else familiar. He crouched next to the narrow bed, nose flared. He reached under and pulled out a hoodie. The sleeve was cut to ribbons and splashed with red-purple blood. Kcaz smelled the fabric. The blood was his.

Kcaz's ears twitched. The door clicked shut. He could hear the hum of a weapon set to fire.

Kcaz turned, his shoulders filling the cell. The narrow length of the room had him caged like a bear. He was on his knees and holding a bloodied rag.

Demi stood against the door, a humming URG-18 in her hands. She was so small to Kcaz, like a mouse to an owl, but she was the one with a particle cannon. Kcaz saw a bandage around her wrist where his claws had cut her.

"I thought you'd be at the club," said Kcaz. "They said you were enjoying a martini."

"It was pretty easy to send another clerk in my place.

Nobody at the club would know the difference," said Demi. "Did you send me there out of kindness or to keep tabs on me?"

"For once, I actually did it to be kind."

"That really sucks."

Kcaz narrowed his eyes. He had no way of reaching her in time to stop her blowing out his chest in a hail of blood and burning meat. He thought about the vehicles destroyed in the raid and imagined how his corpse might look in comparison.

"So, what—Chiba was just a way to get me off your trail? Maybe see if she'd kill me?" asked Kcaz.

"Yeah, she had the reputation. I guess I was wrong."

The shadows of the blinds moved around the room as a passing airship hovered through the canyon. Lines scattered across Demi's determined face.

"How'd you pay for the URGs?" asked Kcaz, needing one last detail to get it to all fit.

"I was saving up to go home...I used all on the URGs," she adjusted her grip. "In for a penny, in for a pound."

"And all this was for what? Selling the platinum bit by bit until you had enough to go home? You could have just kept saving and taken a convoy back."

"And go home as poor as I always was?"

So that's what it's all about, huh? Escaping life in a subterranean dystopia wasn't enough, she wanted more. She had it better than most in the mountains, but she felt compelled to use her connections and risk everything for more. Kcaz didn't have an answer to her question. He had returned here after seven years. Seven years before everything had gone bad. He had to start over with nothing. Chiba had been correct. Any crime Kcaz had committed in his mercenary life always ended in a promise of whiskey. He deserved all the pain and lies that came his way, but he dealt with them sober, as much as it sucked to do so.

"Going to shoot me, Demi?"

"Yes."

She had tried to get Chiba to take care of Kcaz. When that failed, she'd tried to knife him in the subway, but that failed too. Demi's determined expression was a ruse. He could see the terror she felt and was trying to hide.

"Then why are you hesitating?"

"Shut up!"

"I know why," said Kcaz, rising from the floor, filling up the lines of neon light. "You're no criminal mastermind.

You're just a girl with enough intelligence and connections to pretend to be. Put down the gun."

She didn't. Her hands began to tremble.

Kcaz knew he was playing for time to think of a plan. She had already taken a swipe at him and murdered the outcasts in cold blood. She was going to pull that trigger. Kcaz just needed the time to clear the distance. He thought about throwing the bed into her. Would it shield him from the railgun or just give him a more painful death?

"You're not some CorpLord or clan boss. You're not the kind of mastermind I hunt for. If you surrender, I can get you an easier sentence. I can—"

"Shut up! Get back on your knees!"

"If I can find you, then so can the police. They just take longer," said Kcaz, he slowly lowered his hands. "Put it down. Let's go talk to the DarkHarts. With some persuasion and promises, they might even recruit you. They do that with successful threats; it benefits them. They bring former enemies into the fold. That's why they keep winning."

"I don't want to work for the clans! I want to leave this fucking place! You know what it's like, leaving the sun behind, living where the pollution fills your lungs. I saw all of Lizza's contacts, all those connections she made. She never used them. She was a noble's daughter, sent to make a buck. She died here and I was left alone. Now I get to leave once I deal with you." He reached for the bedframe, but realized it was bolted to the floor. She began to squeeze the trigger and Kcaz knew he was about to die.

The door slid open. The light from behind Demi revealed a mid-heighted figure. Demi twisted. A blade flashed and Demi screamed. Kcaz dropped to the ground, his face smashed against the floor. The railgun went off in a blinding flash and blasted through the window, vaporizing the glass.

When Kcaz looked back up, Demi was on the floor. She was screaming and clutching her wrist. Her hand had been sliced clean off. The limp fingers still clutched the weapon on the floor.

Casey Chiba stood in the doorway, a bloodied katana in her hand. Her yellow, wolfish eyes glared from beneath her hooded brow.

Kcaz rose. "Thanks, Chiba."

"Fuck you, Skry." Chiba leaned over Demi, pulling her up by her uniform. "You bitch. You tried to frame me. You sent *him* after me." Demi whimpered in response, tears of pain streaming down her mousy little face. "You fucking traitor. Lizza put her neck out for you. She brought you here for a better life, and this is what you do?!"

Demi bit back her tears. "Lizza dragged me here. I was her household; I didn't have a choice. I was her servant. Then she died and I was left here! Too much bother to bring me home!" she spat. "Fuck you, Chiba."

Chiba dropped her. "Lizza told me to protect you if anything happened to her. She protected you from all of this." The samurai shook her head. "I hope the clans flay you alive." She glared at Kcaz. "You know how I knew Lizza was really dead? I was in the car when she died. We got hit by a drunk driver. I got some new scars from it, but she got crushed. Sucks, but it's as simple as that. When you visited, I knew this one been playing a game she wasn't ready for."

Chiba turned to leave. "Be seeing you, Skry."

Kcaz rose to his feet. He dug a nail into his ear, clearing it. "Be seeing you, Chiba."

The samurai left, leaving her victim bleeding on the floor. Kcaz sighed and took a towel from the bathroom. He wrapped Demi's wrist. "Let's get you to the Medica." She swore as he lifted her like a toy doll. "Try white-collar crime next time."

◆

The door to Kcaz's office clicked shut. He sighed before taking off his coat and hanging it and his hat on the hook. He turned on the radio. He was ready to sleep for the next twenty-four hours, if not longer. The payment from the DarkHart Clan had come through and would cover his rent for the next two months.

"This is Armistice 97.2 and here comes some Peggy Lee! *Why Don't You Do Right.*"

He made himself another cup of coffee before reclining in his chair. It had been a long investigation. *Too long.* He sipped the cup, letting the music wash over him. The smooth vocals usually helped his mood, but the lyrics weren't doing it for him today. He checked the drawer once more; the bottle of whiskey still sat undisturbed. Inviting. Threatening. *One more day.* That was his tactic. Just focus on surviving each day.

Demi had been quiet when the authorities came to the Medica. Kcaz had no doubt she was walking to her execution. *Just another one eaten by the Underground. Poor girl.* Demi had been desperate to leave this place. She was barely more than a child. A reckless one with too many connections, an infectious idea and a big stomach. Kcaz would call the DarkHarts after some rest and help her. *Why should I?* She would have shot him. *Maybe it's just the right thing to do.* Sometimes that was as hard as staying sober.

Boss Dekar's voice crackled in Kcaz's mind. "Are you investigating this because a pack of outcasts got duped and you're bringing the mastermind to justice? Or because they stole from the clans?"

Kcaz didn't have an answer. He didn't know the outcasts' names. He didn't know where they came from or what had led them down this path in the first place.

He sighed.

Sometimes you just got to ruin someone's day. Sometimes it's your job and you just got to grin and bear it. Sometimes in order to survive down here you have to ruin others' lives. Sometimes you just have to be the bad guy in someone else's story. Sometimes you have to be a little evil.

He opened the drawer again. Looked at the whiskey. Closed the drawer again.

Someone else had been like that...and *he* had destroyed everything they had. And for what? For his own reckless greed. Kcaz had been his accomplice in those bad days.

The phone rang, ripping Kcaz from his dark thoughts.

"Hello?"

"Skry! Don't you dare hang up! If you don't get to the Central District's attorney office in the next thirty minutes, you'll be fucking held in contempt and charged with slander, assault, and conspiracy!"

"Who is this?!"

"Samantha Mae McCarthy! Get your big green ass over here!"

Shit.

Kcaz gulped down the last of the coffee from his mug, slammed the phone down on the receiver, and threw his coat back on. It would take at least forty-five minutes to get there. *This'll be fun.* The door slammed behind him.

FROM BELOW

"I don't care," said Finn.

"Why not?" said Gildrec. "Don't you care about your Dvergr brothers and sisters? About all of our people?"

"I care about paying my rent. Now, come on."

Both dwarves walked through the catacomb tunnels. The low stone ceiling and rounded walls made Finn feel like a mouse stuck in a lead pipe. The only sound was the thud of their heavy boots on the floor; their steps echoed down the tunnel.

Finn Stonebjorn wore a blue armoured cuirass over a quilted tunic, an axe-shaped tool used for excavation hung on his belt. In his right hand he clutched a drum-fed submachine gun. His other arm held a plasteel riot shield. He and Gildrec protected the labyrinth of tunnels leading into the Underground. Once it had been a noble duty amongst Dvergr; now tunnel guards were underpaid, overworked, and in constant danger. Thousands of dwarves, humans, and others across the Underground did jobs like this to make ends meet.

The headlamps on their visored helmets made a twin pair of circles that scanned the barren tunnel.

"I'm just saying," said Gildrec. "We work for a security company owned by goblins. Protecting a CropCorp owned by goblins…which helps feed the Underground…which is ruled by goblins!"

"*Everything* is owned by the goblins."

"Yeah, don't you think that's fucked?"

"Will you just shut up!" hissed Finn. "I'm trying to listen."

"We're in a tunnel."

"Yeah—and the next chasm, I'm shoving you in it."

They continued walking through the tunnel, which seemed to never end no matter how often the dwarves had walked them before. The two of them were patrol guards for the Greenfen CropCorp. They spent their days protecting the maze of tunnels and passages that led to the GrowHouses that fed the Underground.

They eventually reached the end of the tunnel; it opened into a huge hall. Immense Dvergr pillars reached up from unimaginable depths. A catacomb plaza the size of an arena spread out before them. The hall was flanked with titanic statues of dwarf warriors, matrons, and smiths.

"~K-Team. Come in.~" crackled a voice through the radio.

Finn tapped the receiver. "Finn here. Go ahead."

"~We have seismic activity due south of you, a depth of three hundred feet. Sector six.~"

"We haven't felt anything." The silence that followed made Finn hold his breath. It could have been a collapse, a tremor, or something much worse.

Finn looked at Gildrec. The other dwarf's frown was visible through his impressive beard; he kept his facial hair long, properly braided, and oiled, with a gold Tor's hammer clasp decorating the central braid.

"~G-Squad is on its way, Finn. Proceed with investigation. Over.~"

"Alright. Over." Finn sighed. "Come on."

The pair of dwarves moved toward a set of steps near the edge of the hall. They'd been through these areas a dozen times before.

Localized seismic movement, thought Finn. The very thought of it made him shudder. The dread draped over him with cold fingers; his heart drummed within his armor.

The two stout dwarves were an island of light in the ruins of their own ancient civilization. The stone eyes of the statues seemed to watch them as the pair passed. The stone floor of the plaza was covered in a thick buildup of dust, but occasionally you could see the murals beneath. Grand images made up of thousands of coloured stones. Battles, wonders, marriages, and oaths. Dwarves over anvils or at prayer, kings on thrones, throngs on the march, armies in battle against dragons and thunderbirds. The history that was taken from them.

Gildrec let out an audible sigh.

"What?" said Finn.

"Just thinking." He was staring up at the statues. "Our people carved the mountains in our image over the course of a thousand years. They built all these amazing things and now we're occupied by goblins."

Their visors met.

Finn sighed. "I know why you care so much. I *do* care. It's just…it's life. It's been a hundred years since the goblins took over; it could still be another hundred before our people get dominion back."

"We shouldn't have to wait that long. We should fight to get our rule back now."

"*Life* is the fight," said Finn. "It's hard enough keeping a job and paying rent, with or without the goblins." He patted his partner's shoulder. "Come on. We have a job to do. And, for your information, we'd still be doing this job even with Dvergr sovereignty."

They reached the edge of a sheer drop into darkness. Their headlamps were unable to reach the distant walls. Finn exhaled; he'd been here before but the anxiety never left him. The impossible black depths surrounded him. Below, a series of narrow switchbacks led downwards.

As they descended, a clatter echoed in the distance. Finn froze, his senses straining through the impenetrable darkness. The only sound he could hear was Gildrec's breathing.

Gildrec stopped a few steps above Finn. "What is it?"

Finn stared for a bloated minute, but there was nothing. He shook his head. "Come on, The quicker we're in, the quicker we're out."

They continued their descent deeper into the catacombs of their ancestors. The stairwell took them to a long bridge. It was incredibly narrow and had no railings. Traditional Dvergr style always assumed the dwarves would be greatly outnumbered in any fight; bridges were designed as chokepoints.

The pair were specks on the bridge, their lights cast out into darkness. Finn caught glimpses of skyscraper-sized pillars and immense faces carved into the stone, great ancient structures of Nyrvellir. He couldn't shake the feeling of being watched.

The bridge opened onto a courtyard the size of a football field. The headlamps illuminated the broken domes and buildings that encircled the plaza, centered on a ziggurat temple to the Aesir. The place should have filled Finn with pride, but it was just another dead city buried deep below. Along the walls of the structure were tributes to the mountains and the gods, Tor, Odinn, Siff, and Frer. Lower still, nearly at eye level, were the Dvergr immortals, Torin, Thror, Dvalin, and Dvela. Finn felt the warmth of his Tor's hammer necklace within his vest. Finn wore it out of habit, not piety; it reminded him of his father.

The pair entered a cracked dome through an arched entrance. Inside, the stone pillars had cracked and fallen to pieces, caving in the dome. The walls were carved with images from the old epics. Finn wondered why archaeologists and archivers weren't down here more often to record everything.

Maybe they just don't care, he thought. No money in digging up old Dwerg stones…

"Woah," whistled Gildrec, craning his head to stare

up. The dome was decorated with a once-stunning twelfth century mosaic of the nine realms.

Turned out there were many more realms in the end.

Finn set down his shield. He tapped the radio. "K-Team calling Headquarters. You reading?"

The radio crackled, but nothing came through.

"We're in too deep."

"Damn fools knew they were sending us out of range," said Gildrec. "We should go. There's nothing down here."

Something scraped against rock.

Finn whipped his head back. The circles of light from his helmet scanned the fallen pillars. There was nothing but long shadows.

"We should get out of here," said Finn as he picked up his shield.

"Agreed."

The pair was hurrying back to the entrance when the entire chamber began to quake, the ground vibrating beneath their boots. Debris fell from the shattered dome. The mosaic walls cracked, ancient carvings crumbled. Finn used his shield to keep balance.

A shard of rock fell toward Gildrec. Finn sprung off his feet, knocking his partner aside. The rock shattered where Gildrec had stood; a crack crawled to the center of the chamber, splitting the mosaic of old Dvergr wars with the jotnar. The floor crumbled inwards, collapsing into black nothingness. The beautiful images melted into the abyss.

When Finn looked down, he caught sight of a moving wall of rocky ribbed skin.

"A wyrm," concluded Gildrec immediately.

"Yeah," said Finn. "That would explain the seismic activity. I thought they didn't come this way anymore."

"Not unless something drove it here."

Finn met Gildrec's visor. "Tor help us."

Static crackled through the radio. Finn glanced back. In the distance, back near the top of mountainous switchbacks, were a dozen more lights in the dark. The reinforcements from the other squad had arrived.

"G-Squad, come in," said Finn.

"~We see you, K-Team. Brokk here. What the hell was that? Over.~"

"Wyrm. A big one, over."

"~Shit.~" said Brokk, gruff voice crackling over the

radio. "~Stay there. We're on our way. Over and out.~"

Gildrec peered downward into the pit. His helmet light reached as far as it could, but it wasn't enough. Small stones continued to fall into the hole, vanishing into the dark, making no sound. "It's bottomless."

"Oh, there'll be a bottom," said Finn.

"Finn!" hissed Gildrec.

Finn looked up. On the far side of the pit, among the shadows of the destroyed pillars, a pair of eyes stared back.

Finn raised his weapon. He licked his lips, trying to perceive what had found them. He had known they were being watched. Gildrec gulped, pumping the charging handle on his SMG against the rim of his shield.

"Show yourself!" barked Finn.

"Just shoot it!"

A second pair of eyes opened in the shadows, then another, and another. From every shadow, crack, and crevasse around the temple, beady eyes were staring back at them.

Finn's stomach dropped. He could feel his heart beating in his ears. He slowly stepped backwards towards the entrance.

Finn heard a scraping sound below his feet. He cast his light down to find the pit lined with hundreds of enormous rats. Several hissed, wincing at the lights.

Not just any kind of rats—ratmen, hunched bipedal rats with spindly little hands that gripped the walls. They had beady eyes and narrow pale faces, their patchy fur was plagued with sores and bald spots. The light of Finn's headlamp glinted off metal knives, belt buckles and scraps of armour. Bone shivs, rusted hooks, and spiked bits of plastic completed the weaponry of the army of rats.

It was an attack on the GrowHouses. A raid for food, supplies, and flesh.

The scraping grew into chittering, excitement spreading through the swarm as they scaled the walls.

Something clicked.

Gildrec had pulled the pin on a flash grenade. They never carried lethal explosives, too dangerous. Flash grenades had their own risks, but in moments like this they were vital.

"Run!"

He dropped the grenade.

They bolted out of the temple. They had to get to the far end of the bridge. White light erupted behind them, and their ears rang deaf.

When Finn's hearing cleared, Brokk yelled over the radio. "~What the hell was that, K-Team?~"

"Rats!"

Finn whipped around, weapon aimed. From every crack and fissure across the temple swarmed countless black figures. Every inch of stone was covered in chittering ratmen.

"Gildrec! On my shoulder." Gildrec ran past, stopping just behind him. Finn squeezed the trigger and his SMG blazed hot lead, cutting into the swarm.

Then they switched. Each took a turn, firing before moving back. They kept moving under cover, reloading when necessary.

Gunfire lit up the ratmen. The dwarves couldn't even see how many they killed; the dead were immediately overtaken by the swarm. It was like shooting into water. Finn and Gildrec switched off, giving each other the seconds needed to clear the courtyard and reach the bridge.

Finn saw G-Squad crossing the bridge from the opposite side. They hurried, headlamps jerking back and forth through the darkness. Finn pulled out his own flash grenade.

"Gildrec! Run! Now!" He pulled the pin and tossed the grenade. A flash grenade was devastating to the sensitive ears and eyes of the rats. The burst of light and ringing noise gave a momentary halt to the horde of ratmen.

Finn and Gildrec reached the bridge. Their boots clattered against the stone as they passed two herculean statues of Dvergr Berserkers. At the curved crest of the bridge, K-Squad formed a shield wall.

"What the hell did you do!" roared Team-Leader Brokk, pulling the pair into the rear rank. Brokk outranked Finn. He was grey-bearded, with a wide face beneath his visor. His nylon sergeant patch on his uniform gleamed.

"Found vermin, sir," said Finn.

"Tor save us," he hissed. "Light 'em up!"

Finn and Gildrec formed up into the shield wall— twelve dwarves in total, four across and three deep. Shields shuddered as the front line locked together, their SMGs set against the rims.

They were a tiny beacon of roaring light against a sea of encroaching shadow. The ratmen attacking the bridge were shredded by gunfire. Clouds of red mist replaced chittering creatures. The instant one ratman was gone, more took its place. The ferocity of their attack overtook the dead and cast aside the weak. Corpses and screaming rats fell off the bridge into the abyss below. As the frontline's weapons emptied, they were handed already loaded weapons.

"We need support!" roared Brokk over the radio.

The radio crackled, but there was no answer. Brokk met Finn's eyes. *We're fucked.* They both knew it.

A clawed hand reached up from underneath the bridge, long yellow nails scraped against one dwarf's ankle. Finn brought his own boot down, snapping the invading limb like a twig. The rat shrieked, falling into the abyss below.

"They're coming from underneath!"

Brokk crushed a limb under his boot. "Forget the guns! We're doing this the old way! Flash!" Finn lobbed his last flash grenade over the shields. There was a bang, and then a burst of burning rats fell off the bridge like matches falling into a well.

The firearms clattered on the stone, kicked off the side of the bridge. The dwarves drew their axes and picks. Finn kissed the blade of his axe.

"For Nyrvellir!" roared Gildrec.

Finn met Gildrec's eyes. Maybe he was right. Their people were under occupation by the goblin clans. They were down here while the goblins and their bosses were up there eating caviar and drinking wine. Dvergr warriors were left to patrol the tunnels while goblins ruled from the halls of dwarven ancestors. The ballads always told stories of the Thanes and Jarls leading their clans into the deeps to fight filth like this.

What were the dwarves now? They were a shadow of their former selves, forced to live under the control of the green-skinned creatures who had stolen their empire. The vermin were the kings now.

"For Nyrvellir!" the squad roared.

The wave of rats smashed against the shields; Finn pressed his shield into the back of the warrior in front of him. The dwarves dug in. Axes snapped and chopped at the rats, blood and brains plastering their shields.

Finn reached over the front with his axe and cracked open a rat's skull. Bones snapped, flesh tore, nails and daggers scrapped against plasteel shields. The dwarven shield wall was an immovable stone against a black tidal wave.

Brokk yelled over the radio, "We need support! We need support!"

The radio crackled, but there was no answer.

"We're out of range!" hissed Finn. His axe crunched bone.

"On my mark!" yelled Brokk. "One step back! Now!"

The wall grunted and took a step back as one. The ratmen drove forward, but were met again with shields and biting axes. Finn saw another paw reach up from beneath the bridge. It grabbed the ankle of a dwarf. Finn crushed the arm underfoot. Three more paws reached up and pulled the other dwarf off balance. He teetered and fell into the abyss, screaming until he was too far down to hear.

Finn roared and joined the front line. His vision became nothing but shadow, glinting steel, and gnashing teeth. Metal daggers glanced off his helmet and claws scraped against his shield. He chopped blindly, over and over again, splitting bones and shattering skulls.

"Step back!"

The line moved back. Another dwarven scream echoed as another fell to their doom. Finn chopped and bashed. His movements became pure instinct. Blood sprayed his face, slicking his beard. A jagged hatchet cracked against his helmet, rattling his head and shattering a headlamp, leaving less light for the squad.

The line slowly retreated across the bridge, the wave of rats failing to break through the dwarven shield wall. A dwarf slipped and was dragged into the horde, screaming as he did, vanishing into the fur and yellow teeth. The twelve dwarves were whittled away to seven.

Brokk joined the frontline, stabbing and slashing with

a short sword. Thin clawed limbs flew. Finn's bracers and sleeves were torn, and he bled from a dozen bites and scratches. A crude knife was lodged into his cuirass. He was hot and sweaty within his armor, blood and flesh sticky on his gloves. The warriors had retreated to the far end of the bridge. Finn crushed a chittering head under his boot. Another attacked and he chopped through a ribcage, spilling pink entrails onto his front.

Brokk stabbed through a rat's mouth, slashing sideways through its cheek and into another rat. He roared into the radio. "We need help! Base! Confirm! We're under attack!"

The radio crackled, but again, there was no answer. If the line broke, they would be slaughtered, swallowed by the horde. Finn chopped at an arm reaching for Gildrec's throat.

The open channel crackled. "~Defensive line formed in sector three. Prepare for raid.~"

Sector three was almost a mile away through winding tunnels. It was a defensible location; that was where headquarters would hold. It was the most effective way to protect the GrowHouses, but it also meant leaving G-Squad behind.

Finn's jaw slackened. *Left behind.* Abandoned. Brokk swore a curse at their superiors. Another dwarf, wishing it would all be over, dropped his guard and allowed himself to be dragged into the horde; his face vanished into rats the size of children.

"What do we do now?" roared Finn to Brokk as he cleaved through another rat.

"I don't know!" He slashed his short sword, disembowelling three more.

There was a rumble, and a tremor shook the bridge. The ratmen paused, ears twitching. A ratman with a banner and cutlass squealed. Within seconds the rats clambered away, the sea of them disappearing into every crack and shadow.

The dwarves stood alone at the bridge. Five had survived. Finn's arms trembled; his gear weighed down on him. He wiped his visor with the back of his glove to clear fluids.

"What the hell was that?" hissed Gildrec.

The tremors shook again, even more violently this time. Gildrec's arms wind-milled; he was on the edge of the bridge. His eyes met Finn's before falling over the side. Finn reached out, screaming, but it was too late. Gildrec was gone.

Behind the squad, rock exploded in a pillar of debris. From within the earth rose a titanic wyrm. Its length was unknowable, but it was as thick as a school bus. Its tri-jawed head snapped one of the pillars into rubble. Its skin was like corrugated stone.

Along a section of its flank was a gaping wound, black and cavernous. The edges were shredded like it had been chewed at by a thousand razors, exactly like the damage to Finn's armor. Finn gasped, *the vermin did this. They planned it.* They had driven the wyrm into a rampage for their attack.

The squad was helpless against something of this size.

The wyrm's immense bulk broke the bridge they stood on. Finn watched as the lights from the squad quickly disappeared around him. Finn closed his eyes. He hoped Valhalla was real. Then this might have been worth it.

But not this. Not a pawn in a goblin's game. No.

He felt the bridge give out under him, and he started to fall.

♦

Finn gasped and spit up water. He ripped off his helmet, and cold air touched his face. His beard was matted with grime and his clothes felt soaked. He could hear water lapping up against him. He groaned and sat up. It was completely black, as if his eyes were still closed.

He unlatched his cuirass and let it clatter down beside him. He could feel the blood on his arm had coagulated. His head rang. He got on his hands and knees and dry heaved. When he recovered, he pulled out a glowstick from his tunic. He snapped and shook the rod, letting the low glow illuminate his surroundings. From what he could tell, he was on the edge of a subterranean lake. The rock around him was slick as glass and felt just as sharp.

Stay alive. He found his axe. He sighed in relief, finding safety in the simple weapon. He pulled himself out of the water and stood up, raising the illuminating rod. He couldn't perceive more than the shore of rock and the black water.

He rubbed his head, feeling the ache in his brain. He had survived. Whether through the blessing of the gods or simple chance, he had fallen into water and instinctively reached the shore. He had survived and that was what mattered.

A familiar grunt sounded near him.

"Gildrec!" cried Finn. He dashed to the side of his friend. Gildrec's legs were covered in tiny pale crabs picking at his flesh. Finn used the axe to scatter them away.

"Gil! Come on!" He pulled his friend to his chest. Gildrec's helmet was shattered, his visor cracked. A fissure in his brow bled down his broad cheek. His leg and arm were both at unnatural angles. Finn tried to rip the cuirass free, but Gildrec groaned from the pain. His ribs were shattered within his armor. Gildrec wasn't going to make it. They were in too deep.

"Finn," wheezed Gildrec. "Don't." He tapped the Tor's hammer. "Don't forget. We. Are. Dvergr."

"I won't forget. I will never forget." The goblin clans had left them for dead. Had left them to their certain doom. "You were right. You were right. We can't live like this."

A smile touched Gildrec's lips. Then his body shuddered and his arm went limp.

Tears fell down Finn's cheeks. He pressed his forehead against Gildrec's. *I will never forgive. I will never forget.*

Finn could hear the splash of water echo nearby.

He turned, but the light from the glow stick was too dim. He felt for the flare gun on Gildrec's belt. It had survived the fall. Finn raised the snub-nosed gun and fired. The burning ball of light rose, then floated slowly downward.

Finn stood up, axe in hand.

He stood on a tiny island in the centre of an immense cavernous lake. The shores were covered with piles of dead rats and the remains of G-Squad. The walls dripped with moisture. The water reflected dull red from the phosphorus flare. The glassy water stretched for miles in every direction, marred by the occasional bobbing rat body. Jagged rock formations dripped with perpetual condensation. Mountainous spires of rock poked up from the water and drooped down from the ceiling.

Finn saw a series of craggy rocks leading from the island to the gaping maw of what looked to be a tunnel at the far end of the lake. It felt as if he was on the edge of an ocean, alone.

The flare died when it touched the water, shutting Finn back into darkness with nothing but the low eerie light of the glowstick.

"I will never forget," said Finn to the darkness. "I will never forgive. The old grudges will be made new and the goblins will know Dvergr vengeance."

The water splashed. Finn turned, both hands gripping the axe.

From the water rose a pale white crustacean the size of a car. A shrimp-crab hybrid with claws as big as shields and a segmented tail curled under its back. Its periscope eyes were blind, but a dozen twitching antennae sprung out from its horizontal mouth.

It snapped its claws and began crawling toward Finn. There was another splash and another pale monster rose out of the water. Another chittered on the island, having begun feasting on Brokk's broken body. Another stepped out from the mountainous pile of ratmen corpses.

"I will never forget. For Nyrvellir!" He grit his teeth and charged the creature.

SLAY THE BEAST

Ava stood on the forest trail, looking up at a pine tree. It was bent downward, not by gravity, but some unnatural magnetism. Other trees around the trail also leaned inward, their needles falling to the ground like feathers.

This can't be good, thought Ava.

She followed the trail up a slope, mountains growing in the distance as she walked. *Into the foothills of the Appalachians again.* Her black cloak and hood wrapped around her, her hand never leaving her holster. Her longsword hung on her hip. The rugged terrain and mountains reminded her of her battle against the dwarves of Skerhol. An unpleasant tingle crawled up her spine. *I can handle this. I can handle a monster.* She had handled far worse already.

The half-moon was high in the night sky; the black pines reached up from the hills like sentinels. The wind tasted wrong. The trees rustled the wrong way.

The flutter of wings drew her attention. On a high branch sat an owl, dirty grey with fluffy legs. Its head rotated, a third eye blinked, and it flew off again. Mutation. Magic mutation. Norwich had taught her plenty about that—the danger of magic, its infectious nature, its reality-warping power.

Ava headed for a lodge at the crest of the slope. There, her contact, a local ranger, would meet her.

She had been hired to hunt down a monster, a monster that had infected the local area with magic.

She had spent the last two weeks wandering central NeoAnglia, looking for work. The local lord, or rather his sixteen-year-old daughter, had offered Ava this job despite the bounty on Ava's head. The village was desperate.

The lord had told her the lodge had been abandoned the previous year. A flickering lantern in the window light told Ava that her contact was waiting for her.

She was about to step onto the porch when she noticed something in the dirt. Kneeling, she traced her hand over a four-toed footprint. She looked back up and saw huge claw marks in the lodge's door.

Shit.

She drew her pistol from its holster, cocking the hammer as she entered the lodge. The smell was overpowering, flies already buzzing over the mess.

The lantern in the lodge flickered shadows across the remains of the dead ranger. Poor bastard. It looked like the ranger had tried to defend himself. Ava could see his rifle and several spent cartridges on the floorboards. Blood pooled across the boards. A leather bag rested on a chair. The ranger's eyes were open wide with terror beneath the goggles of his gasmask, staring back at Ava. His head was the only part of him that remained intact. The rest was a gory mess. His spine and ribs exposed, pink and grey organs strewn about, clothes ripped to shreds, limbs sprawled out at unnatural angles. The ranger held a hatchet, clean of blood, in one hand. *Christ, he didn't even have a chance.* The way he had been eviscerated...he must've died immediately, but the monster kept ripping him apart long after.

She took the bag from the chair against the wall. Inside there was another gas mask and a heavy black vest. *Must have been for me.* Magic infected everything, one would need protection in order to survive deeper in the forest.

She put the equipment on. The vest was heavy, lined with lead, offering little physical protection, but hopefully some against the magic. She rewrapped her cloak around herself and picked up the rifle, along with any bullets she could find. She took the lantern too.

She exited the lodge and stood at the crest of the slope. The path led down into a densely forested valley filled with old growth, knotted trees, dense bush, and gods know what else.

The lantern illuminated a pair of dragonflies as big as falcons that landed on a nearby tree. Their wings and legs were warped with magical mutation.

Ava could taste it in the air—that rotten, electric taste, like spoiled milk and buzzing static on her tongue. She pulled down the gas mask, adjusting the straps until it fit properly. She breathed in and out slowly, clearing her airways of the rancid taste, before venturing into the valley.

She had a beast to slay.

Following the trail, Ava went deeper into the valley. She raised the lantern, peering through the interlaced columns of trees. Pine trees bent at odd angles, but there were far more wondrous and terrifying things to see than that. The wind had died down, but the trees continued to sway.

There were insects bigger than birds, mutated and warped, that flew through the air or clung to the flora. Ugly, veiny mushrooms grew nearly as big as the surrounding trees. Ash and oak gnarled, stretched and bloated. Sheets of crusted moss clung to boulders like coral. Amongst the strange and bizarre grasses, grew bulbs of furry fungi, their fleshy stalks glowing and swaying in the non-existent breeze. There were birds with extra pairs of wings that made them look like butterflies, squirrels with two heads and bundles of fluffy tails, a dull grey stag with flowers sprouting from its antlers. Everything mutated in unnatural ways. All around, the magic infected the forest.

Ava reached the bottom of the valley, finding a stream between the rocks and fungi. The water bubbled, flowing clear over the stones. She kneeled, setting down the lantern. She took a stick and poked it into the water. The stick curled and warped as if it was burning, growing stems and bulbs from a completely different plant. It was as entrancing as a lit match. She threw it aside, wiping her hand on her shirt. It felt wrong. Everything here did.

She heard a small crash and snapped to attention. A rhino-beetle as big as a cow entered into her view; it carried itself on stretched out spider-like legs. It continued on through the forest, grazing on mutant fungi, disinterested in the little human.

Another shuffle. Ava whipped around with the rifle, knocking the lantern off a rock. Shit! It shattered in the water, shutting her into darkness.

In the low moonlight, she saw something crawl out of a bush. Some poor mutated animal. Whatever it *had* been, it was now unrecognisable, only a hobbling tumor with various unmatched pieces to drag it along. A goat head brayed, choking on phlegm as spider legs and a cat arm clutched a rock. Its naked flesh pulsated; its eyes glowed a sickly green.

Ava grimaced and considered shooting it to put it out of its misery, but it disappeared into a bramble of bulbs. Ava exhaled.

"Hullo?" A voice came through the darkness.

Ava froze.

Was that my imagination?

"Hullo…?" said the voice, again. A man's voice.

Ava waited in silence. The minutes drew out longer and longer until the regular hum of the forest returned. Ava was crouched behind a mutated tree. She peaked around the trunk, rifle at the ready, but saw no one. She crept between the mutated foliage until she came to a clearing. There she took cover by a boulder and she scanned the area.

A camouflage UTV was parked just off the trail, engine and headlights shut off. Antennae, a dish, and various other equipment stuck out from the back of the chassis, a wide trailer connected at the hitch. The door was etched with a heraldic emblem, the words *Oceanic Institute of Miskatonic University* beneath it.

Ava saw a figure in camouflage coveralls. He wore a

full-face gas mask connected to a backpack respirator. He kneeled by a tree covered in moss growths, working with a knife to gather samples. Over his shoulder was slung a gas-rifle, and he had a handgun on his belt. An electric lamp sat next to him, casting light across the ridge.

Ava slid back behind the rock, considering her options. *He's doing research on the creature*, she concluded. *He is doing what he thinks is right, I guess.* Ava had been hired to kill the beast and she needed the goddamn money. She wouldn't hurt him if she didn't have to. *He's only doing what he thinks is right.*

She checked the rifle's mechanism before working the bolt. Loaded and ready, she stepped out from behind the boulder, weapon aimed at the man. She got within two meters of him before she let her presence be known with a cough. He turned from his samples and froze. Green eyes were visible through his mask, widened with shock. He raised his hands, dropping the knife and a plastic container of samples. "Don't shoot! Don't shoot!"

"Who the hell are you? Did the Rutens send for you?"

"They did," he said, looking from the rifle barrel pointed at his face to Ava. "They didn't like that I was researching the beast. I knew they'd hire a slayer."

"I'm not a slayer," said Ava. *Just a woman who needs*

the money. "Tell me where the creature is." *Be scary.* "And maybe I'll let you live."

His eyes narrowed, studying her, but through masks it was quite the standoff. The mutated forest ebbed, flowed, and pulsed around them. Unnatural energies were trying to infect them the way they had infected the forest. "No you won't," he said. "You just want to kill the creature. You don't want to kill me if you don't have to."

"That a fact?"

"You'd have shot me already if it was your intention. Please just put down the gun," said the man. "My name is Irwin Green, I'm a graduate student from Dunwich. They didn't have anyone else so they sent me to investigate. I just need to get some information on what it's done to the forest first. The forest can heal. The creature just needs to be relocated. It's the water—"

"I don't really care," said Ava. "If you haven't noticed, it's dangerous. It'll kill you too."

"Most animals kill," said Irwin. "It's in their basic nature, a means of survival. That doesn't mean they need to be exterminated. And this one is unique. I don't know if it's a mutation, an anomaly, or something else. We won't know until I get it out of here. Come on," he pleaded. "We can work together. We can get it out of here."

He wanted to save the creature so desperately.

The locals wouldn't like it though. They may not even pay Ava. Her stomach growled and her eyes were heavy. She hadn't had a decent meal or sleep in weeks. The last thing she ate was some cakes and a cup of tea she had been served at the local lord's estate. *I need this kill.*

"Come on," said Irwin. "We can do this together."

Ava lowered her rifle. "You're right," she said. He lowered his hands in response, exhaling, visibly relieved. "I'm not gonna kill you."

Ava whipped the rifle like a club, striking Irwin in the side of the head. He collapsed to the ground, unconscious. Ava kneeled over him, ensuring he was still alive. His chest rose and fell with a constant rhythm. He'd be fine.

"Sorry," said Ava. "I need the money."

She opened the UTV door, threw him inside, shut the door, and left him there to recover while she continued her search.

♦

Ava followed the stream up the other side of the valley. Irwin had mentioned the water. If the creature's radiation had gotten into the stream, it would have been carried downriver, feeding the forest and eventually reaching the town. If this wasn't stopped, the town might begin to mutate like the rest of the forest.

The trail zig-zagged as though the land itself had been stretched like a piece of fabric. Ava looked up, seeing a bird clinging to a fungal tree with talons that grew from the elbows of its wings. It squawked, bioluminescence rippling through its feathers, then flew off. Ava turned, watching it disappear into the night.

As she ascended the trail she was met with more displays of the magic's infection. Dust was falling from up above, uninfluenced by the impossible breeze that swayed the trees. Dust? No. It was ash or snow floating downward. She'd seen magic in Norwich, and again with a magician in Steigford, but this was different. This was something far more powerful. Whether it was evil in nature or not, she couldn't guess. *Maybe it just is, and that's what is terrifying about it.*

A pair of rocks flanked the stream at the apex of a ridgeline. They had gathered irradiated materials like sediment from the water until they grew into a demonic gate.

Something hit Ava's foot. It was a limb, a sheep's leg. The bone was visible through white flesh matted with blood. It reminded her of her purpose. She had a beast to slay. Ava checked the rifle's mechanism before hopping over the water and through the unnatural gate into a wide clearing.

The stream originated in the mountains above, but here a pool formed. A pool ringed with oblong waystones and twisted trees. The pool was a deep blackish-green. Rocks warped by the intense magical energy became swirled obelisks at the water's edge. A mutated bird flew by, long like an eel with dozens of feathers along its body; it glowed blue and illuminated the area. The ground was covered in pebbles, debris, and the strange ashen snow falling from above. Ava could see bones that had been chewed clean, bits of tools, weapons, and torn clothes scattered around the glen. The very bark of the trees was swirled into the likeness of brushstrokes.

The darkness of the night wrapped around the pool as the mutant bird passed into the distance. The only remaining light was a low glow that surrounded the waystones—dim, but enough to see by. Ava licked her lips; she could hear her breath in her ears. She knew the creature had to be close. Everything seemed to radiate outward from here. Here the magic was at its most intense. Her gloved fingers tapped the grip of the rifle. How would she flush it out?

She kneeled by the water. Remembering the stick from earlier, she didn't even think about touching it with her hands. It felt like leaning over the edge of an abyss. The pool was a well of pure cosmic energy. The old stories of cursed wells and ancient portals must have come from places like this. It was never a god's token or pit of despair.

This was an open nuclear reactor, pulsing with impossibly dangerous powers.

She picked up a rock and tossed it in. The ripples danced across the glassy surface.

After a long moment, the rock landed back in front of Ava with a splash. The top of the rock face swirled, melting like wax, and then reformed. She licked her lips, tossed another rock in, and waited for it to splash and land in front of her. It did.

"What do you want?" she whispered.

She picked up another rock, feeling the weight of it in her hand. She stood up, holding the rifle at her hip. *Come on.* She exhaled, letting her body lose its tension, becoming fluid like water. *Come and face me.* She hurled the rock in—a splash, and then nothing.

She aimed with the rifle, her eyes searching.

The rock shot out of the water and over Ava's shoulder. She fired into the water, worked the bolt, and fired again. She unloaded the five-shot magazine into the water. Each bullet vanished with no effect.

"Come on," she hissed between her teeth. She reloaded the rifle. Her eyes darted across the pool to the surrounding trees. The hum of the forest quieted.

A splash came from across the pool. Ava fired. The bullet whistled into the distance.

Shit.

She worked the bolt, scanning the pool. Another splash, another missed shot. *Come on.* She moved to another waystone, taking cover and working the mechanism. She had killed monsters, bandits, and knights. She had battled dwarf rangers, magicians, and curses. She could kill this thing. She just needed to find it.

She peered around the stone, eyes darting around the pool from shadow to shadow, stone to stone. *Nothing.* She broke cover, keeping her back to the closest stone while slowly and delicately creeping to the next.

A splash echoed on the opposite side of the pool. Ava fired. The flash from her gun illuminated a crooked body. *Got you.* She fired again, as quickly as she could, but the second flash revealed nothing. *Where are you?*

She pressed her back against a stone, reloading as she searched.

The forest's hum returned, surrounding her. The bioluminescence of the animals and plants rippled with low blues, reds, and yellows around the pool. Ava could see pairs of eyes in the branches and fungi above, glowing like tiny candle flames.

Heavy, scraping footfalls drew her attention. A huge form strode between the trees, little more than a shadow in the dim light. It was tall and crooked, a heavy tail trailing behind it. It stood upright on long wolfish legs.

"Got you." She raised the rifle and fired, but when the flash subsided, the creature was gone. As if it had never been there in the first place.

She backed up toward another waystone. She needed to come up with a plan. Ava's eyes darted, searching.

Two crunches sounded behind her. Her stomach sank.

Ava whipped around, swinging the rifle, but scaly, clawed hands caught the weapon, hands with two fingers and two opposing thumbs. One hand wrapped around her arm and one around the rifle. Ava looked at the tiny yellow eyes staring back at her. Her body acted by instinct; she wrenched her arm free, the claws scraping her forearm.

She drew her sword in a wide slash with her free arm.

Ava's swing threw her off balance when it connected with nothing. The rifle clattered against the rocks. The creature was simply gone. Vanished. Disappeared.

She groaned, looking at her arm. Deep gashes cut into her flesh, hot blood dripping from her elbow. Ava gripped the sword with both hands, falling into a low defensive stance.

The trees were empty now, quiet. All the eyes that had been there moments before had disappeared. Fear crawled up her spine, her arm throbbing.

"Come on! Where are you?" she roared.

Claws scraped against stone behind her. She whipped around, sword ringing off the waystone with a burst of sparks, but the beast had vanished again. It was toying with her. "What the absolute fuck," she hissed. She clenched her fists tightly around the hilt.

Pebbles clattered to her left. She attacked but found nothing but air.

Bushes rustled on her right. She attacked but cleaved only through empty foliage.

I need to get out of here. Ava needed to retreat, reassess, and try again. Could she afford to? She was hungry, exhausted, and desperate. If she retreated, the beast would have time to recover in its home territory and Ava would be the one on the run. *I need time to think, time to plan—*

The shadow stood between two mutated pine trees, staring at her with yellow reptilian eyes. Clawed hands hanging at its side, it stood with its backward-bent legs wide, head lowered like a cat preparing to pounce.

"Fuck," said Ava.

She bolted through the trees and down the slope.

Carried by her momentum, she flew over logs and the stream, past boulders and bloated fungi, taking swift strides as she crashed through the forest. Branches lashed at her face and she tore through a curtain of ivy. Ava glanced over her shoulder. The creature was running on its hind legs; Ava knew she wouldn't be able to outrun it.

She tried to head it off, swerving through the uneven terrain toward its path. The beast crashed through a tree, bursting the trunk in a cascade of wood chips. Ava hissed, leaping out in front of the next tree, sword at the ready to take the charge.

It was gone. Vanished. Bits of debris floated to the ground; slabs of fibrous wood clattered around her feet.

"What the—?"

The beast leaped out from behind another tree and slammed into Ava. She was knocked off her feet. Air rushed from her lungs, her chest wrenched, and she lost grip on the sword. Blinking through the pain, she looked up. The monster stood over her, black, slitted eyes narrowed.

Ava drew her revolver. "Fuck you." She unloaded the chamber.

The monster stood above Ava. The bullets fired, flash

illuminating its scaley hide, but connected with nothing. They whistled off into the distance.

That's not fucking possible.

The creature hissed, inhuman and completely feral. The bioluminescence of the forest ebbed and flowed in streams around the beast. It looked weirdly familiar, almost a mix between reptile and human. It had a short snout and forward-facing reptilian eyes, but overall a vaguely human visage. Along its cheeks and forehead were a complex series of markings and fissures, almost like tattoos. Tiny, frilled ears vibrated as it chirped. It leaned down over Ava and opened its mouth slowly. With a sudden snap, its bottom jaw split at the chin. A maw of razor-sharp teeth opened up to devour the woman.

No. Not now. She stubbornly, desperately, refused the creature its kill. She drew a knife from her boot and slammed it into the monster's thigh.

The blade shattered. Steel was useless. Bullets were useless. The monster pounced and Ava rolled away just in time. She picked up a slab of broken wood, using it as a shield to give herself time to think. She caught the beast's mouth and claws on the length of timber. She pressed against its impossible strength, arms straining and heels digging into the forest floor.

How the fuck am I going to get out of this? She grimly

concluded that she had gotten in way over her head. This wasn't a band of dwarves or mercenaries, this was a cosmic beast. This was far beyond her understanding.

But someone else understood it.

Over the beast's shoulder, Ava saw a figure running towards the battle. She gasped, pushing against the monster. Irwin Green, his mask and coveralls shining in the glow of the forest, hurtled towards them.

"How the fuck do you kill this thing?" Ava screamed, her strength fading.

He raised his rifle and a pop sounded.

A feathered dart struck the monster in the bicep. It whipped around, hissing with its detached jaws.

Ava leaped away, dropping the timber. The beast shook its head furiously, trying to clear its vision. Its shoulders sank, the sedative beginning to work through its system.

It roared and charged toward Irwin, bounding on all fours.

"How?" yelled Ava. Nothing she had used worked. Her bullets had passed through the creature like it was a ghost.

"Silver!" Irwin leapt over the stream, narrowly avoiding

the creature's blindly fast charge. The side of a fungal tree burst in a cascade of fibers.

"Silver?" She glanced at her sword on the ground. The crossguard set with leaping wolves sparkled in the unnatural light. She snatched the weapon by the blade, half-swording, ready to use the silver hilt as a crude hammer. Her Master had insisted on a diverse training regime, one which included old Saxon styles of wielding a longsword. She bolted toward Irwin.

The monster disappeared behind one tree and reappeared out of another, leaping to attack Irwin with its scything claws. Ava leaped into the attack, hammering the crossguard into the creature's head. It connected. The monster tumbled, barreling into the stream. It pushed itself back up, hissing, eyes blazing with fury. Its back and tail were lined with webbed spines

Irwin and Ava stood together. He fired his gas rifle, striking another dart into the beast's shoulder. It hissed before crawling away, disappearing behind a boulder.

Ava and Irwin turned to stand back-to-back. He reloaded his rifle. "Last dart."

"Only three?"

"These can drop a theropod. It should only need one or two."

"This *thing* isn't normal."

He laughed through his mask. "You don't say?"

Ava held her sword defensively. "How the fuck is it doing it? It's like a ghost…or it's teleporting."

"I don't know," he said. "But if I can trank it, I can get it out of here."

They waited, their eyes searching the forest. Ava's heartbeat hammered in her ears and the forest hummed around them. The glow of magic came in waves and the trees swayed with the flow. Ava watched the flow of it, noticing a ripple disturb the waves like a rock dropped in water.

The creature burst into view, leaping for the pair with jaws wide, claws out, and eyes blazing. Ava swung the sword, holding it as tightly as she could. The silver crossguard connected and struck it in the head, knocking it off course. It tumbled and slammed into the base of a tree. Irwin fired the gas rifle; the dart hit the beast in the flank.

The beast tried to push itself up, but its limbs quivered— the sedative was finally taking effect. Its eyes struggled to hold their fury. Its hissing call choked and its movements became sluggish. Its eyes flickered.

Ava raised her sword over her head, readying to finish it off.

It hissed, jaws and fin-ears flaring in unison.

"Don't!" said Irwin. "Just leave it."

"I was hired to kill it. So that's what I'm going to do."

"You were hired to remove it. Let me take it, you can claim the bounty."

Ava gritted her teeth, holding her high strike in place. "I'm going to need proof. I need its head, or something. A scale or hand won't do." The creature held her focus, its rage dragged down by the sedative. It was nearly four meters long, nose to tail, a monstrous reptilian humanoid with fin-like spines down its back.

"Then I'll pay you!"

The creature made an intoxicated swipe at Ava, but she easily dodged it. The markings on its face extended down its back in a complex design. It reminded her of a circuit board, or a series of roots...maybe a bit of both. Its growls grew sleepier and its eyes dulled.

"You'll take it away from here?" said Ava. "Make sure it can't hurt the people or this forest?"

"The forest will heal, it will take time, but it will heal."

She didn't need to kill this thing. *I don't have to kill*

everything, she thought to herself. A lot of things on the Wrong Side needed to die, and a lot of things deserved it. This was a creature whose presence had a powerful effect on its environment, but it couldn't help its nature. She sighed, letting her sword lower to her side. "Fine."

Irwin stood next to her. "Will you help me get it out of here?"

"For a day's wage. *Your* wage."

He laughed. "It's not as good as you think."

She chuckled, their masks facing each other. He may have been handsome...it was hard to tell. "I'm just trying to survive like everyone else."

He nodded, kneeling next to the creature. He pulled a device from his belt and adjusted its dials. It made a clicking sound. He waved it back and forth, the clicking swelling into a squeal. "I can't tell where it came from, but this creature is not natural. Nothing natural produces this much MR-2."

"What?"

"Magus Radiation - Type 2."

"So it *is* radioactive?"

"Sort of," he said. He reached into a pouch, producing a vial and some tools. He scraped the creature's scales for samples. "It will need analysis. If it's a demon, it would have been summoned. If it's an anomaly...then something else..."

As he touched the tip of a blade to the creature, the beast shuddered. Irwin fell backwards. The creature's eyes opened. It made the sound of a cat purring. The sound grew until it reverberated through the entire forest. Ava felt it in her chest. Light glowed from the creature's eyes until they were pure orbs of bright yellow light. The light ran down the markings on its face and followed the fissures along its back. Its spines stuck straight up, the markings glowing and pulsing like data streams or synapsing neurons.

The light blazed and the smell of burning metal filled the air. Ava felt the taste of magic on her tongue grow to a numbing buzz, climbing into her skull until her brain was rattling. The forest howled with light and sound. Irwin crawled back, raising his arm to block the light.

Ava shielded her eyes too.

The light and noise peaked, and then it all darkened.

The creature was gone.

The bioluminescence throughout the forest extinguished with it. After a long moment of quiet, Irwin stood up, brushing himself off. "Fuck." Both of them stared at the empty hollow where the creature had been. Irwin looked at his device, adjusting the dials once again. After a long moment, he chuckled to himself and holstered the device. He unhooked the seals of his mask, letting it fall around his neck. He *was* handsome.

Ava followed his lead, removing her mask and shaking the strands of sweaty hair away from her face. She breathed in the clean, clear air. The forest would heal. The hazy taste of magic was gone.

"Want to get some breakfast?" asked Irwin, smiling at her.

"Only if you're buying."

"You *did* knock me out," he rubbed the side of his head.

Ava shrugged in response.

As they walked, she looked up at the sky. The pale moon was huge against the jet-black sky. She grimaced, feeling very small in a world full of things she had no way of truly understanding.

Fuck, what else is out there?

THE FLEET'S REVENGE

The ocean was an endless plain of rolling black hills, the clouds a charcoal veil as far as the eye could see. The wind blew hard, whipping at the flags at the masts' tops. Ten mismatched vessels cruised in a triangle formation. Searchlights cast out into the darkness, cutting through the night like giant fingers.

David O'Malley held the rail of *Merlin*'s wheelhouse hard enough for his knuckles to go white. Ocean spray bit at his grey sideburns, his face red and hard from decades of sailing on the water. He scanned the dark tides of the Atlantic coast.

The makeshift fleet had launched that morning, in search of the beast that had sacked their town. It had killed and feasted on their family, their friends, and their neighbours; when news arrived that there would be no real aid from Dunwich or Grandton, the surviving townsfolk knew they had to take matters into their own hands.

A monster had raided their town, a primordial devil from far beyond the waters of NeoAnglia. Krakens were common, and serpents not unheard of, but this beast, this Terror, was different.

O'Malley saw that the darkness grew more intense to the south toward Malnack Island, the last place they had to search for the beast.

He re-entered the wheelhouse. Willard stood at the helm; the thin man was as hard as nails, and as angry as the rest of them. His dour face studied O'Malley. He had been *Merlin*'s helmsman for years.

"We'll find it," said Willard. "Storm's coming." He didn't say it as a question.

"We've had storms before," replied O'Malley. "This time is different."

Willard nodded; his eyes glanced to the deck below. Two volunteers had joined their crew of three. One was a peddler from Grandton who had been on vacation with his wife; she was lost when the Terror stormed *through* the motel. The other was a dwarf, a smith from another village who had come down for the first proper summer weekend of the year.

Boy did he pick the wrong weekend.

The volunteers fumbled with the necessary duties around *Merlin*; the old tug boat had seen better days. The peddler—O'Malley thought his name was Lovejoy—nearly fell off the deck when they hit a wave, but managed to save himself by the skin of his teeth.

"They shouldn't have come," said Willard.

"No," said O'Malley. "But we needed the bodies and they were eager." They'd all lost something to the attack of the Terror.

O'Malley glanced at the console next to the wheel. Pictures from years gone by were plastered above the screen. His calloused fingers touched a photo of himself and a younger man holding up prized tunas, smiles on their faces. Next to that was a wedding picture of the younger man with a beautiful woman, and next to that was a photo of a baby boy.

I'll get it. I'll fucking get it.

They had all lost someone in the Terror's attack. Now it would feel their vengeance.

♦

After the attack of the Terror, a third of Brightfall's businesses and buildings were damaged, nearly a hundred people dead and injured. Brightfall had been humbled by hurricanes, bad touring seasons, smaller fish stocks, fuel taxes, and quotas. Their town had struggled over the decades. They were used to hardships, but not like this.

This was different. Not just in the sheer carnage, but in the exactness of the cause. A monster unlike any other had attacked them.

After four days of doing their best to clean up the destruction, Lord Roland Joyce called a town meeting in one of the surviving halls along the waterfront. Fishermen, farmers, lodgers, and strangers from the outlying area had come. Some came to offer aid, some just to see the damage, shrug and move on, and others came to exploit the situation.

O'Malley sat in the first row near the front - he was an elder and respected fisherman.

Lord Joyce stood behind a long table. The few house guards and aides flanked him, a fortified wall of bodies.

Lord Roland Joyce was a pudgy man in a too-large suit, his black hair flat on his head and whiskers bristling around his babyish face. He looked like a child playing at ruling a town. He was the inheritor of duties once held by better men.

O'Malley had known Joyce's father. *Now that was a man worth offering fealty to.*

"Good people of Brightfall," began Lord Joyce, speaking out to the crowd. "As soon as this disaster befell our fair town, I sent word to our king and any of his vassals with the capacity to aid us. It's with most gracious appreciation that—"

"Oh, just fucking tell us," howled Noah Payne, another fisherman.

Would they send food? Supplies? Engineers to rebuild?

We need the navy, thought O'Malley. *We need to kill the Terror before it returns.*

Lord Joyce huffed with indignation and continued reading from his document. "Dunwich has heeded our call and is sending an expert from Miskatonic University to assess the situation and advise on the proceedings. They are someone familiar with beasts of this nature. They will likely arrive today."

An expert in monsters, thought O'Malley.

A shudder went through the crowd, mutters of confusion,

disappointment, and most of all, anger. Long had Dunwich and Grandton left the small corners of NeoAnglia to fend for themselves, paying them no attention except to collect tribute. Brightfall was a forgotten corner of small folk, too small to be a travel destination, too poor to be worth any investment. And now, when they truly needed help, the king was to provide…nothing.

It was only the latest in a long line of insults.

O'Malley rose.

The Lord sighed. "Something you'd like to say, Mr. O'Malley?"

O'Malley pursed his lips the same way his eyes narrowed. "You'd have us wait while that beast lingers off our coastline?"

"I do as our king bids."

"What of us?" said O'Malley.

"When the expert—"

"No, *my* Lord Joyce," hissed O'Malley, hating the taste of the words as he said them. "We will not wait. We're the ones the world forgot about. We've called for assistance the last three winters and received *nothing*." O'Malley's anger grew as he continued. "We've lost everything! Our families, our homes, our lives! And you're just as much to blame as the king!"

The murmurs grew into shouts of agreement.

"The Terror is ours to kill and we will not wait!"

A chorus of roars followed.

"I launch as soon as the tides allow!"

The crowd burst into whoops and cheers.

A single piercing sound cut through the noise: nails against a chalkboard. The crowd hushed and winced at the sound. The bodies parted to reveal a woman sitting on a chair.

"You're all damn fools," she said, wiping the chalk from her nails before reaching into a bag of chips. "You'll all die if you run out like blood hungry idiots."

O'Malley glared. "You think so, Regina?"

The woman was a short, solid sailor wearing a trench coat. Regina Claiborne, Captain of Tartarus. She was the last remaining Kraken hunter in town. On her hip was a sickle-sabre. Her short grey hair hung around her face in a mess of dagger-like bobs. Her jaw was set on edge, hard as unpolished granite.

"If you damn idiots think swarming the Terror will bring it down, think again. Bunch up your tackles, tangle your nets. You'll be running into each other. You don't send a school of fish after a shark. You send another hunter...a single, precise hunter."

O'Malley laughed. *This woman wants it all for herself.* "And that'll be you, Regina?"

She shrugged.

"No, Claiborne, tonight *I* get to kill the beast."

"You can try." She looked through the crowd to Lord Joyce. "For three thousand dollars I'll kill this Terror. Let an *expert* handle it."

Lord Joyce didn't look compelled by either option.

He's just so weak, thought O'Malley.

O'Malley scoffed and stormed out of the hall. Willard followed him out. O'Malley shoved past bodies. He had much to do to make the *Merlin* seaworthy and ready for battle. He would be the one to kill the monster. No one else would get the chance. He would make it pay for what it had taken from him.

♦

The fleet of rickety fishing vessels and pleasure schooners arced southwest. Lightning flashed in the distance; it took several long seconds for the thunder to reach the fleet. A storm was a curse for sailors the world over, but tonight it didn't matter. Tonight was different.

The radio crackled. "*The Danube* here. O'Malley, I

don't like the look of this. Let's reel it in and try again tomorrow."

O'Malley ripped the radio from its port. "Listen, damn you, if we don't hunt this bastard we risk him attacking again. We don't stop until the Terror is killed. Got it?!"

The radio crackled with a meager. "Aye…we'll keep going."

Several more "ayes" came from the other boats, ten in all. *Merlin, The Saint George, Leviathan*, and *The Queen Beatrix* were the only local fishing vessels that had survived the attack of the Terror. *Leviathan* had lost its captain, but her captain's widow gave the vessel to another who had lost his ship in the attack. The remaining six vessels—*Hornet, The Danube, The Daniel, Crusade, Annsor*, and *The Caw*—were all pleasure boats. Bay boats, cruisers, and cuddy cabins, the lot of them. O'Malley was shocked *The Hornet* and *Crusade* had survived this long.

The fleet continued outward, deeper into the night. The triangle stretched back as O'Malley pushed *Merlin* harder. The vessels on the flanks lagged behind. *There might be an advantage* in that, thought O'Malley.

He pulled up the radio. "This is *Merlin* calling in *Annsor, The Caw*, and *Hornet!*"

The open frequency chirped with awkward affirmatives from the three captains. They weren't real captains. Two were Grandton accountants, one was a peddler from Dunwich. O'Malley glanced back at *Hornet* and saw the peddler struggling to answer the radio while trying to keep his boat moving straight at the same time.

"The three of you, split off," he ordered. "Like hounds, weed out what you can. Call us if you see anything."

The captains for *Annsor* and *The Caw* peeled off. The triangle formation stretched into an awkward W-shape as the wings rushed forwards. Their tiny squealing motors were barely enough to fight through the thrashing waters. *Hornet* had fallen further behind and refused the order. The peddler from Dunwich was struggling.

Let him, thought O'Malley. *Man spends too much time counting dollars and too little pulling rigging.*

O'Malley chewed his lip. Lightning crashed again, this time much closer. The thunder vibrated the windows of the cabin. The rain pattered harder, like pebbles being pelted against the plasti-glass.

Willard made a sound like a balloon wheezing air. O'Malley shot a venomous look back at the helmsman.

The fleet carried on deeper into the storm. The sea grew choppier; the fishing vessels bucked and swayed, their bows frothing with white foam. Their engines roared under the strain.

The other sailing vessels lagged hopelessly behind; *Hornet* was almost a league behind them now. Its flapping canvas dragged the vessel back.

The fool didn't know when to reel it in, thought O'Malley.

O'Malley watched the horizon, nearly invisible in the darkness between lightning strikes. With their current heading they would be entering the shallows soon. *Merlin*'s searchlight swerved left to right, scanning for the distant shoreline.

Soon...thought O'Malley. *The Moby-Dick to my Ahab. I will kill the Terror.* Lightning webbed across the sky, the clouds as thick as black wool. The thunder felt immediate.

The radio crackled on an empty frequency.

"Has anyone seen *Hornet*?" called one captain.

"Lost sight of her!" responded another.

O'Malley snatched the radio and put it to his mouth. "Fallen behind. Let them. The Terror awaits."

"Aye," responded Captain Archibald of The Saint George. Other affirmations came from *Leviathan, The Queen Beatrix,* and *Crusade. The Saint George* was the core of the formation, the heaviest tanker with the longest hull. Its deck was filled with survivors armed with rifles and deck pikes. They hunted no mere kraken; this was something far worse, and they would need every advantage. *Leviathan* and *The Queen Beatrix* had a surprise for the beast too.

O'Malley slammed the radio into its holder. Confusion, then anger covered his face when he saw the compass on the console. "We're off course you damn fool!" he roared at Willard.

The thin man stood frozen, doe-eyed, just staring at O'Malley.

"Move!" O'Malley shoved the thin man aside and took the helm. His calloused hands gripped the metal wheel. He threw the throttle forward.

A voice called over the internal system. "You're pushing it too hard, sir!" It was Nox Nimor, Merlin's engine technician of two years.

O'Malley ignored it and forced *Merlin* back on course. The remains of the fleet followed behind as best they could. The horn of *The Saint George* blared, their engines pushing the heavy ship through the thrashing waves. The bay boats on the flanks fell further behind.

"We can't push like this!" crackled *The Danube* over the radio.

The lightning crashed, then thunder that shook the cabin. Through the rain O'Malley could make out the jagged, rocky point of Malnack Island.

Where are you? Thought O'Malley. He pictured the beast in his mind: its long snout, interlocking teeth, and vivid red eyes.

The radio crackled. "I'm turning back! We'll try again tomorrow!" It was *The Danube*, one of the pleasure boats. O'Malley glanced to the starboard side to see the open-top speeder peel off from the formation. The boat's white chrome hull slapped against the water as it swerved back in the direction of Brightfall.

"Cowards!" screamed O'Malley over the radio.

The radio crackled again, but nothing came through.

"Did you see that?" crackled from *Crusade.*

"What?" said O'Malley. His head dashed down the lines of the fleet. *The Danube* was gone. One moment it was there, then it was gone…foaming surf swirled where it had been.

He looked back toward the bow. His eyes snapped wide. Oh no.

O'Malley screamed over the radio. "Break off!"

Distracted, he hadn't noticed the sandbar. *Merlin* bucked and halted, the engine squealed as it drove deeper into the shallow sand. Willard was knocked off his feet,

O'Malley barely held on.

The radio crackled. "*Merlin*! We need help!" It was *Crusade*.

O'Malley howled at Nimor to cut the engine. He rushed out of the wheelhouse, grabbing the rifle that hung by the door. The wind and rain slammed into him, pattering against his jacket. He wiped his eyes before looking back at the fleet in horror.

The remaining ships had peeled off and avoided the sandbar, but now everyone was scattered. O'Malley could see thrashing lamps and chaotic spotlights whipping in every direction. They were vulnerable, unable to support one another in the dark of the storm.

"O'Malley!" shrieked *Crusade*.

The small trawler in the distance was arching on its port side. Its spotlight thrashed back and forth. The ship bucked on its side. Over *Crusade*'s deck rose a huge monstrous paw, webbed between the digits. The scything claws cleaved right into the deck. Metal squealed. Men rushed around the deck with weapons. A second hand rose over and dug itself into the wheelhouse.

The entire boat bucked with the immense weight of the Terror as it pulled itself up. Like a child climbing awkwardly onto a paddle board, the Terror's immense arrow-shaped head rose out of the ocean, streams of water falling down its head and shoulders.

Crusade's crew rushed forward with boarding pikes and handguns. Flashes of gunfire illuminated the night. The Terror backhanded the crew off the rear of the trawler, shearing off sections of the ship's deck.

It roared, crawling up the boat and pulling it down into the depths. The boat began to sink. Archie Snyder, a man O'Malley had grown up with, stood atop the remains of the boat's wheelhouse. He screamed inaudibly and fired an AR-15. The blaze of gunfire illuminated the monster's horrible visage, a prehistoric demon, the progeny of long-lost evolutionary timelines.

The Terror pawed away at the gunfire. It opened its huge jaws, its interlocking teeth stretched wide. A spout of red flames engulfed *Crusade*'s crushed wheelhouse. The fire was a beacon in the night. The ship's hull crunched and it sunk down into the water. The fires quickly extinguished, plunging the battlefield back into stormy darkness.

The fleet swerved around to engage the beast.

The Terror dove back into the water as the other ships arrived, a mushroom cloud of white foam rising high in the air. *Leviathan* and two other speeding boats circled the wreckage, their searchlights probing the black water.

O'Malley wanted to scream at them. *They're looking in the wrong place!* But first he had to get *Merlin* out of the sand.

Willard had already called The Saint George to haul them out. *Merlin*'s crew stood along the rail with hooks and ropes tied to the gunwale. *The Saint George* was coming at an angle so its crew could toss the lines and swerve back out. It was risky. They were short on time.

O'Malley was at the rear of *Merlin*, his boots doing their best to grip the rain slick deck. The men on *The Saint George* were calling, ready to toss the lines. O'Malley glanced up, surveying the surroundings.

Annsor zoomed towards where *Crusade* had perished. Suddenly it bucked, the tiny speeder skipping across the waters like a thrown stone. Its hull cracked in the center. Several of its crew were thrown into the water. When the small boat regained its balance, the Terror erupted into view and smashed *Annsor* into the water.

The Caw, Leviathan, and *The Daniel* circled the monster. Men fired rifles and pistols in a tri-facing broadside. Some threw sticks of dynamite that exploded in pillars of white foam.

The Terror must have been standing in the shallows; it was chest deep in the water. It spun its great head and shoulders to face its enemies. Men screamed and hooted, firing their weapons, shining lights at the monster. O'Malley could see its long, interlocking jaws, its blue-black snout, and deadly red eyes. Streams of the men's blood poured down its jaws; it pawed at the gunfire, angered by the attack.

Until *The Caw* got too close.

The Terror twisted around with its jaws open. The men screamed as a pillar of fire engulfed the bow of *The Caw*. The men dove into the water. *The Caw* sped by, carried by momentum and burning like a pagan funerary pyre. *Leviathan* sped away, rejoining *The Queen Beatrix* in deeper water for their plan. *The Daniel* was left alone in the shallows to battle the monster. The Terror dove into the water, swimming for the cruiser. The Daniel arced around, fleeing from the monster. The Terror pursued, visible only as a ripple in the black water.

We're losing. O'Malley forced the thought from his mind.

The men of *The Saint George* tossed the lines to *Merlin*'s crew, who tied them down immediately. O'Malley gripped a rope and with mechanical precision tied it to the rear rail of his boat. The timing had to be perfect. The Saint George arced back out to sea.

O'Malley jumped back as the lines snapped tight.

Merlin jerked backwards.

The dwarven blacksmith wasn't so lucky. His legs were caught in the line. He screamed as the immense pressure cut into his legs, slamming him into the gunwale with bone-breaking force. Willard tried to pull him out.

Idiot Dwerg. O'Malley left them. *There's still a battle to win. A monster to slay.* He went back up to the bridge.

"Nimor! Fire her back up!" said O'Malley.

The engine roared to life.

O'Malley looked through the rear window.

The Daniel had fled away from the shallows, then began circling back to reengage. That was their mistake. The Terror rammed the ship, puncturing its hull. Huge claws dug into the deck, pulling the monster's head over the railing. Men screamed and battled, but were killed or forced to abandon ship. The ship crumbled into the depths with the Terror on top of it.

With a horn blow, two jigs charged the beast, spotlights blinding its eyes. Strung between *Leviathan* and *The Queen Beatrix*, submerged half-way in the water, was a huge chain net. The beast turned, roaring fire through the net.

The chain net slammed into the Terror, entangling its

arms and jaws. The monster roared in frustration as it was wrenched from the sinking corpse of *The Daniel*. The pair of jigs dragged the immense beast through the water. It thrashed and struggled, a spout of flame flying recklessly upwards, its tail whipping in and out of the water.

With *Merlin* free, they could finish this. O'Malley screamed out the window, "Cut the lines!"

Willard cut the lines with a boarding axe and the freed dwarf collapsed onto the deck, screaming, a gory red line across his hamstrings.

O'Malley threw the throttle forward and spun the wheel. *Merlin* arced away from the sandbar and toward the pair of ships. *We have him. We have him!* The surviving boats— *Merlin, The Saint George, The Queen Beatrix*, and *Leviathan*—were all old fishing vessels. All the pleasure boats had already been destroyed. *So few against this devil.*

It's all we need, O'Malley thought to himself. They were all old guard sailors and fishermen: real proper seamen. As O'Malley guided his ship toward the beast, he looked back to the photos at the console.

He touched one of the photos, his son holding up a prized fish. *He would have been thirty-one this winter.* He had never lost the dimples in his cheeks or the curl in his brown hair. *The best pieces of me before I got old*, thought O'Malley. His son had had a young wife and a young kid, a toddler who would grow up without a father. *They would be avenged. We will all be avenged.*

The two jigs, *Leviathan* and *The Queen Beatrix*, bucked over the waters. They were small, but ruggedly powerful vessels. Smoke poured from their engines as they tried to haul the beast toward the rest of the fleet. The net shuttered.

The Terror stood on its hind legs, its clawed feet digging into the seabed, its bulk criss-crossed with the chain net. It roared and gripped the chain net with its blubbery arms. It pulled the jigs to a halt. The falling rain pelted its white front and blue-black shoulders. Lightning flashed behind the howling beast, its interlocking jaws creating sawblade silhouettes against the light. It roared and poured a spout of fire over both ships. Fire spilled off the decks like molten metal and flames lapped up the cabin, scorching the hulls. Men on fire screamed and jumped into the water.

Both ships melted like balls of wax and vanished into the depths. Explosions rippled under the surface when the fires hit the fuel tanks. Men thrashed in the water, only for the beast to loom over them, snapping its jaws, leaving nothing but foam.

God. Two left. O'Malley grabbed the radio. "We're going in! We'll try to trap the fucker! Saint George, you come in and ram it!"

Captain Archibald called back. It was a final desperate

gambit. The pair of jigs had failed with the chain net. *Merlin*'s net couldn't be much more use, but it may be just enough to give *The Saint George*, muscly vessel that it was, the chance it needed.

The Terror wadded through the water, its snout fishing out injured and dying men. Screams were silenced with a quick jerk of its head. O'Malley saw the Terror take a man in its jaws and rip his legs off with its claws. O'Malley held his nerve and the ship's wheel.

Merlin circled the beast. The crew met its hellfire gaze as it ripped another man in two.

O'Malley stuck his head out the window and shouted. "Get the net on the starboard side!"

The dark figures on the deck ran to complete their task. The engine sputtered as it was pushed beyond its regular limits. The waters crashed, jerking the boat.

The beast stood ready as the two remaining ships circled like wolves.

O'Malley pulled the horn with three sharp jerks. The Terror turned and roared, wading toward *Merlin*. The boat crashed through the water. O'Malley stared into the burning red eyes of the Terror. He saw nothing but soulless contempt. He threw the throttle as far as it would go, the engine squealed.

The Terror opened its jaws. O'Malley could see it was getting ready to spew fire.

He swerved to the right, avoiding the Terror, and a wall of flames rippled past the tugboat. The arm of *Merlin*'s crane held a wide net. The net caught the beast's arm, tangling in its claws. The boat flew past it, pulling the beast off balance and dragging it back. The Terror struggled back to its feet, but it was unable to regain its balance. It roared and thrashed; it spit flames, but they grew more and more faint.

You're running dry, old boy. O'Malley nearly laughed. *We've got you!*

The Saint George's horn blared. The heavy trawler crashed through the waves. Men on its decks fired weapons or waved boarding axes. The Terror whipped its immense crocodilian head back and forth. For the first time, O'Malley could see fear in its red eyes.

How do you like it, you fucking monster?

O'Malley grit his teeth and turned the wheel, pulling the monster's arm behind its back, keeping the beast off balance.

The Saint George closed the distance to ram the monster.

"We've got him!" shouted O'Malley to no one but himself.

The Terror turned its huge head up, eyes perceiving the crane that tangled its limb. Intelligence sparkled within its reptilian brain. It opened its mouth and let out a tongue of flame, squeezing the last of its reserve. The net caught fire. Cords turned black and snapped. The Terror tore its hand free.

The Saint George barreled toward the beast; the last dozen yards vanished in seconds, but the Terror roared and threw itself on top of the boat, climbing onto the deck with its thrashing tail and digging claws. O'Malley tried to turn the boat around, but a massive wave slammed into the side of *Merlin*. The ship bucked to the side. O'Malley almost lost his balance. Willard and Nimor went overboard. The peddler managed to hang on.

I'll come back for them. I'll come back for them.

O'Malley looked back at *The Saint George*. Flashes of gunfire erupted on the deck, lighting up the monster's long jaws. It moved quickly on all fours, like a lizard. Men vanished inside its jaws. A clutch of orcs charged with their pikes and halberds. They were soundly tossed aside. Captain Archibald stood on the roof of his bridge, a flamethrower in his hands. He had been one of O'Malley's groomsmen thirty-odd years ago. The man had lost his daughter to the pox a decade ago and then his wife to the Terror.

Give 'em hell, Archie, thought O'Malley.

A pillar of greenish fire erupted from the copper spout of the flamethrower. It slapped the Terror in the face, stinging its snout, but it wasn't enough.

The Terror charged on all four legs and crashed through the raised bridge. It slapped Archibald away, sending his dismembered body into the depths.

The Saint George was gone.

The monster slithered off the sinking carcass of *The Saint George,* becoming only a ripple in the water. All became quiet and still.

The Terror had vanished.

No. No. No. No.

O'Malley had failed. He turned *Merlin* around and headed south. The dark waters off Malnack island filled with shipwrecks, debris and bobbing dead bodies. The ramshackle fleet had fought and failed. More lives taken by the monster. This time, however, O'Malley had led them straight into this massacre. He tried to imagine his daughter-in-law and grandson waiting on the beach, looking out to that golden sunrise, waiting for a ship that would never return. *I failed. I failed us all.*

The engine sputtered. The lights in the wheelhouse flickered.

He saw Willard in the water, paddling, waving for help.

The peddler barged into the wheelhouse, soaking wet. "We're running!" it wasn't said like a question.

O'Malley looked back. Willard and Nimor thrashed in the water and other survivors clutched to debris. O'Malley ground his teeth, he knew he had no choice and turned the wheel around. "Get the life preservers!" he roared at the peddler. *Get them. Get out. Get them...*

The engine below squealed and sputtered. *No.* It had been pushed far beyond its limits. It finally sputtered to a stop and the lights went out. *Merlin* was dead in the water.

That's when O'Malley felt the claws scraping against *Merlin*'s hull. He closed his eyes as the force knocked him off his feet and everything became only the snapping of the ship and the ear-splitting roar of the Terror.

♦

A gull cried on the quiet empty beach. The destruction of the Terror attack on Brightfall still smoked and smoldered.

A woman screamed.

O'Malley opened his eyes. The morning sunrise bit

into him. His face was crusted with sand, his clothes torn to ribbons; a crab scraped at his swollen foot. He couldn't remember if he had drifted or swam to shore. He had survived and somehow made it home. He blinked, looking toward the shimmering orange waters and to the wharf, the beach, and the half-destroyed boardwalk.

He pushed himself up, rubbing his exhausted eyes. For the merest moment he thought it had all been a nightmare. Then he remembered how real it was.

All his friends and associates, the regular tourists and passing travelers caught in a tragedy, everyone who had joined his fleet's attempted revenge, everyone who had joined the fight against a monster...All of them...Dead.

He opened his eyes and saw Willard's hollow dead eyes staring back.

He blinked.

Willard's body sat in the surf caught on a buoy. Skull open, arms covered in blackened flesh. A gull perched on his shoulder, ripping flesh from within his ear.

O'Malley blinked again, adjusting his vision. Bodies.

There were bodies everywhere he looked, men caught in the wharf and corpses draped over rocks. Crabs scuttled over the corpses, feasting on the remains; gulls squawked over the pieces. Severed limbs stuck out of the sand

and mangled ribbons of flesh filled the surf, turning the foam pink.

O'Malley let out a wordless scream.

"There's someone alive!" shouted a voice.

Two women rushed to him, pulling him up. He didn't recognize them. They must've been strangers who had recently arrived in Brightfall.

"The beast! The beast!" he screamed, unable to articulate anything else. "It's the devil. The devil itself!"

O'Malley looked to the Atlantic, screaming as he was pulled away by the strangers.

On the horizon, almost a mirage, stood a hulking shadow. The beast surveyed its new territory. Pleased with its good work, it dove back into the ocean. The tyrant monster was content with its prize.

ACKNOWLEDGMENTS

One day I was at work, peeling mangos for sushi and listening to death metal, and my sous chef walked up and said, "For someone who writes and listens to so much dark, fucked-up shit, you're such a cheery guy." To which I responded, "Someone else has to do the screaming." These stories come from a dark place, but it's real and I am better for telling them.

I want to thank Sheldon and Cathy Dyck, Lee MacFarland and James Welbourne, Lesley Lindal-Dobson, Kellie Huyun, Divya Negri, Brianne Michaud, Lyndon Radchenka and Alex Homenko, all of whom help me every day with their encouragement and enthusiasm for me and these pulpy dark fantasy stories. More thanks to the kitchen crew at Earl's St. Vital for their endless support, especially Kat Lapointe and Robert Ashley.

Thank you to my beta readers Ashley Kowalchuk, Tiffany C. Lewis, V.T. Dorchester, Liam Naughten and Jason Shultz, the first ones to start hammering my drafts into legitimate stories.

An immense thank you to Adam Petrash for his insightful and thoughtful editing, G. M. B. Chomichuk for his guidance and gorgeous artwork, Chloe Brown for her hard work and imagination, and Emma Skrumeda for pulling double duty as a beta reader and copy editor—she has touched every piece of this collection and it is better off for it.

Thank you, Mom, Dad, Sarah, Josh, Charlie and Justin. I love you.

Writer. Creator. Geek.

Zachary F. Sigurdson (Z. F. Sigurdson) is a writer from Winnipeg, Manitoba. Born 1995, he graduated from the University of Manitoba in 2017 with a politics degree. Having set aside academic aspirations for creative ones, he has written numerous short stories with several reaching publication.

Interests include reading, writing, schlock moves, fantasy, horror, monsters, dinosaurs and history.

He has worked as a journalist for The Manitoban, as a farmer, as a cook, as a clerk, among other professions.

---

zfsigurdson.com   @ZFSigurdson95   zfsigurdson@outlook.com

Manufactured by Amazon.ca
Bolton, ON